THE BOXCAR CHILDREN

The Boxcar Children Mysteries

THE BOXCAR CHILDREN HAUNTED LEGENDS SPECIAL

Featuring

The Haunted Clock Tower Mystery
1–134

The Ghost in the First Row
135–240

The Sleepy Hollow Mystery
241–355

created by
GERTRUDE CHANDLER WARNER

Albert Whitman & Company
Chicago, Illinois

The Boxcar Children Haunted Legends Special
created by Gertrude Chandler Warner

Copyright © 2016 by Albert Whitman & Company
Published in 2016 by Albert Whitman & Company

ISBN 978-0-8075-0724-7

Printed in the United States of America
10 9 8 7 6 5 4 3 2 1 LB 20 19 18 17 16

Cover art by Anthony VanArsdale
Interior illustrations by Hodges Soileau, Robert Papp, and Anthony VanArsdale

For more information about Albert Whitman & Company,
visit our web site at www.albertwhitman.com.

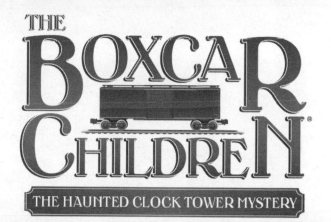

THE BOXCAR CHILDREN®

THE HAUNTED CLOCK TOWER MYSTERY

Created by
GERTRUDE CHANDLER WARNER

Contents

CHAPTER 1

The Tower

"I think I see it!" shouted Benny Alden, pointing out the car window.

"I do too!" called his sister Violet, who was sitting beside him.

"Yes, that's it!" said their grandfather, James Alden. He steered the car up a hill. "That's the famous clock tower."

Benny was only six years old and Violet was ten, but they were on their way to college. Their grandfather was taking them to visit Goldwin University, where he had studied forty years before. He was back for his weeklong class reunion and had brought his four grandchildren with him. Twelve-year-old Jessie and fourteen-year-old Henry looked out the car window too. A tall clock tower loomed over their car and over the whole campus of Goldwin University.

James Alden was the children's grandfather, but he had been more like a father to them ever since their parents had died. At first the children had been afraid to go live with him, because they thought he would be mean. So they ran away and lived in an old boxcar in the woods. But when they discovered what a kind man their grandfather was, they came to live with him in his big house in Greenfield. And he even brought the boxcar and put it in their backyard, so they could use it as a playhouse.

The family had been driving for nearly five hours. Everyone was happy when they finally arrived.

"It's even more beautiful here than in the pictures you showed us," said Jessie, looking at the beautiful stone buildings covered with ivy.

Grandfather pulled into a parking lot. Directly in front of them was the tall, narrow clock tower, ten stories high.

"Can we go up there?" asked Henry.

"Sure," said Grandfather as they all got out. "It will feel good to stretch our legs. From the top you can see the whole campus. I can point out the building where I had my classes, the dining hall where I ate my meals, and the dormitory where I lived. That's where we'll be staying this week."

"How do we get up there?" Benny wanted to know.

"We take the stairs," said Grandfather.

"Stairs?" repeated Benny, craning his neck to look at the top of the tower again. "There's no elevator?"

"No, just stairs," said Grandfather, grinning. "Lots of them."

"One hundred sixty-one, to be exact," said a voice behind them.

The Aldens turned to see a man standing there. He was about Grandfather's age, with thick white hair and a long white beard. He was neatly dressed in a dark suit with a red-and-white vest and matching bow tie. The school colors were red and white, and Jessie noticed his tie was decorated with tiny bears, the Goldwin mascot. The man wore shiny tasseled loafers.

"I'm Ezra Stewart," the man said, putting out his hand for Grandfather to shake. "You must be an old Goldwin student, back for the reunion."

"Yes, I am. And these are my grandchildren." Grandfather introduced each of them.

"Mr. Stewart, how did you know how many stairs there are inside the clock tower?" asked Jessie.

"Because I go up and down those stairs at least twice a day," Ezra said. "I'm the carillon player."

"The what?" Benny asked.

Ezra smiled. "I play the carillon—the bells in the tower. My assistant and I give three concerts a day: morning, noon, and evening. I take care of the bells and the clock as well."

"I used to love to wake up to the carillon music when I was a student here," Grandfather recalled.

"Come on up, I'll show you," Ezra said. "But you have to promise me one thing."

"All right," Henry agreed. "What is it?"

"You must call me Ezra," he said.

"Okay, Ezra," said Benny. "But do we really have to walk up one hundred and—how many stairs was it?"

"One hundred sixty-one," said Ezra. "And you don't have to walk. You can run. I'll race you!" he called over his shoulder as he set off toward a door in the bottom of the tower.

Benny grinned as he took off after Ezra.

The door was made of thick, solid wood. The tower looked as if it had been built long ago. Inside was a narrow, winding stairway. The stairs went around and around in a tight spiral. It was dark because there were only a few lights, and only a few narrow windows cut into the thick stone walls. The rest of the Aldens followed Benny and Ezra at a slower pace. Around and around, up and up they walked. Their footsteps echoed on the stone steps. It was difficult to move quickly in such a tight spiral on the small, uneven stairs.

"This is kind of creepy," Violet said.

"Don't worry," Jessie said. "I'm sure we'll get to the top soon."

A few minutes later, they were standing at the top of the tower in a small room with tiny windows on all four sides. They were a little bit dizzy and slightly out of breath from the climb. Violet was happy to be out of the stairway, although this dusty little room wasn't much better.

Henry went to one of the windows and looked out. "Wow!" he said. "What a view!"

"It is quite spectacular, isn't it?" Grandfather agreed. "I think it's the most beautiful college campus in the country."

"Of course it is," Ezra agreed wholeheartedly.

"What's that big green lawn down there?" Benny asked, looking out another window.

The children all crowded around the window and looked where Benny was pointing. There was a green lawn crisscrossed by sidewalks.

"That's the Quad," said Grandfather. "*Quad* is short for 'quadrangle,' which means a four-sided shape."

Benny quickly counted. "Yes, it does have four sides."

"What's that big building down there with the dome?" Violet wanted to know.

"That's where the largest classes are held," said Ezra.

"And what are those smaller buildings on either side of it?" Henry asked.

"Those are Morrill and McGraw Halls, where I had several of my classes," Grandfather said. "The one on the northern side of the Quad is Morrill; the one on the southern side is McGraw. And it looks like they're building a new building on the other end." He pointed to a building that was still under construction.

"Where was your room, Grandfather?" Violet wanted to know.

"Do you see that big hill?" he replied. "We called that the Slope. The dormitories are down there, and so is the dining hall."

At last the children turned away from the window to look at the room they were standing in. The walls were filled with framed pictures of the university. Many of the photographs were quite old and had a brownish tint.

Just then the clock chimed loudly.

"It's almost time for the evening concert," said Ezra. "Would you kids like to watch me play the carillon?"

"You bet!" cried Benny. "Is that it?" He pointed to the large wooden console in the center of the room.

"Yes, that's the carillon," Ezra said. "The bells are upstairs. We'll go up in a minute so you can see them. They're the best part—you won't believe how big they are."

The children had never seen anything quite like the carillon before. It reminded them a little bit of their upright piano at home. Just like their piano, it had a music stand on the front. Underneath the stand, instead of a keyboard, there were two long horizontal rows of wooden knobs sticking out. Down near the floor was a row of wooden pedals, and up above the carillon was a row of wires leading up through the ceiling.

"How does it work?" Jessie asked.

"You sit on this bench to play it," Ezra said

as he sat down. "When you press down a knob or a pedal, a bell rings. Like this," he said, pressing down on the far left knob. The children heard a bell chime above them.

"That's really neat," said Henry.

"Can I try?" Benny asked.

"Sure," Ezra said.

Benny carefully pressed down one of the knobs in the middle. Again the Aldens heard a bell ringing over their heads.

"Now let's go see the bells," Ezra suggested.

The Aldens followed Ezra out of the tower room. A small dark stairway took them to the floor above, where the bells were housed. There were two rows of large heavy bells on the bottom and two rows of smaller bells hanging above.

"That one on the end is bigger than me!" Benny cried.

"And it weighs a lot more too," said Ezra. "It weighs more than forty-five hundred pounds! Would you like to go inside it?"

Benny's eyes grew wide. "Can I really?"

"Sure," Ezra said.

Benny bent down and ducked underneath

the edge of the heavy bell. When he stood up inside, all the others could see were his legs sticking out at the bottom. "Hello out there!" he called. His voice had a strange muffled sound from inside the bell. Finally he ducked down and came back out. "I've never stood inside a bell before," he said.

"We have forty-nine bells here, which makes this carillon one of the largest in the country," Ezra said.

"So how does the carillon play these bells?" Violet wanted to know.

"Good question," Ezra said. "Did you notice those wires that came out of the carillon and through the ceiling? They come out here." He pointed to the row of wires on the floor next to the bells. "Each wire is attached to a clapper inside a bell. When you press a knob on the carillon, the wire pulls the clapper on the bell." He pulled one of the wires with his fingers to show them. The clapper hit the side of the bell and made a ringing sound. "Each bell is specially made to play a different tone. When you play them together, you can make beautiful music."

"That's wonderful," Jessie said.

"In all the years I was here I heard a lot of concerts, but I never knew how it worked," Grandfather said. "Thank you for showing this to us."

"Would you like to go back downstairs now and watch me play the evening concert?" Ezra asked.

"We sure would," said Henry, speaking for the whole family.

Back downstairs, Violet asked Ezra, "How did you learn to play?"

"I learned a long time ago, when I was still a student here. I practiced on that console there." Ezra walked over to what looked like a smaller carillon in the corner. The children noticed that it had knobs just like the other one, but there were no wires attached. "This isn't attached to the bells, so you can practice without the whole school hearing you. It just rings on these metal plates above." Ezra pressed a knob, and they heard a clanging sound, like a xylophone. "This is where I've taught all my assistants.

"And now I'd better get out my music for the

concert," Ezra said. He began sifting through some stacks of papers on a large desk next to the practice carillon. After a few minutes, he still had not found what he was looking for. He became angrier and angrier. "Where did Miss Barton put it?" he muttered to himself.

"Is something wrong?" Violet asked. Ezra had been so friendly and nice before, and now all of a sudden he seemed like a different person.

"It's this new assistant I have." He sighed. "She's a student named Andrea Barton. I like things to be a certain way up here. After all, I've been doing this for over fifty years— since I was a student myself. After a concert I always put the music back, in alphabetical order, on this desk. There isn't much space up here, so you have to be organized. But she always mixes everything up. Nothing has been the same up here since she started."

"Can I help you look?" Violet asked.

"No, no, no, I'll find it myself," said Ezra, sounding annoyed. "Oh, that girl makes me angry," he said under his breath.

"I'm sorry," said Violet in a quiet voice.

Ezra looked up, surprised. "Not you, dear," he said. "I was talking about Miss Barton." At last he pulled a stack of papers from the pile. "Ah, here it is."

He sat down on the carillon bench and the Aldens gathered around him. After placing the music on the stand, he opened to the first page. Then he began to play. The Aldens watched, fascinated. Ezra's hands, closed into fists, moved rapidly up and down the row of knobs. His hands crossed over and under each other as he pressed one knob after another with the sides of his fists. At the same time, his feet worked the pedals. From above, they could hear beautiful music.

After Ezra finished the first piece, Jessie said, "That looks like hard work."

"It is," Ezra said. "I've got calluses on the sides of my hands." He showed them how his hands had grown tough on the sides he used to press the knobs. "When I first started playing, I used to wrap my hands in bandages and wear gloves. But now I'm used to it."

Ezra went on to play several more pieces, each more beautiful and difficult than the one before. After half an hour, he played a piece the children recognized.

"That's the school anthem, isn't it?" Henry asked. "We've heard Grandfather singing it."

"Yes, it is," said Ezra.

As the hum from the last notes hung in the air above them, the Aldens applauded.

"Thank you," Ezra said, bowing his head slightly.

Just then there was a creaking noise from up above.

"What was that?" Benny asked, his eyes wide open. "I thought we were the only ones up here."

"This old tower creaks and groans all the time," said Ezra. "Some say it's haunted." His eyes twinkled, but his voice was serious.

"I remember those stories," Grandfather said. "The ghost in the clock tower."

"Aren't you scared to come up here by yourself?" Benny asked. "Like at night?"

Ezra looked sharply at Benny. "Well, I certainly don't come up here at night. No one does. Ever."

Chapter 2

A Strange Light at Midnight

After the Aldens left the tower, they picked up the key to their suite and drove to the dormitory.

"That tower was really neat," Henry said as they were driving.

"But a little spooky," Benny said.

"You don't believe there's really a ghost, do you?" Henry asked.

"Um, no," Benny said, but he didn't sound too sure.

"Ezra was just teasing," Jessie said. "He

was nice."

"Yes, he was," Violet agreed. "Except when he was talking about his assistant, Andrea Barton. Then he seemed so different."

"That's true—he said that nothing has been the same there since she started working," Jessie remembered. "He said she messes everything up."

"He did seem like he was very neat and orderly about everything," Henry said. "You could tell by the way he was dressed."

When they arrived at the dormitory parking lot, Grandfather looked up at the redbrick building in front of them. "Good old Sage Hall," he said softly.

"It's about time you showed up!" said a man striding across the parking lot, his arms held out wide.

"Joel Dixon!" said Grandfather as he and the man embraced, patting each other firmly on the back.

"And these must be your grandchildren," said Joel, stepping back to look at them. "Don't tell me. This is Henry, and Jessie, and Violet."

Each child nodded and smiled as Grandfather's friend said his or her name.

"And this young fellow must be Benny," Joel said.

"You've got that right!" Benny said with a smile.

"This is my old college buddy Joel," Grandfather said.

Joel was a large man with dark hair, a friendly smile, and a big belly.

"We've heard a lot about you," Henry said.

"On the car ride up here our grandfather told us about all the crazy things you two used to do," said Benny, grinning.

"Your grandfather and I had a good time, didn't we, Jimbo?" said Joel. The children smiled. They weren't used to hearing their grandfather called by a nickname. "You didn't tell them about the time I lost the key to our room and had to climb in the window—did you?"

"He sure did," said Benny with a laugh.

"Oh, he did, did he?" asked Joel. "Well, then, did he tell you about the time he took some frogs from the science lab and hid them in my bed?" Joel asked.

"You screamed so loud!" Grandfather said, laughing.

Everyone laughed, and Grandfather thumped Joel on the back affectionately.

"So, when did you get here?" Grandfather asked.

"Just a few minutes ago," Joel replied. "I was just coming back to check my car and make sure my son and I hadn't forgotten anything. Don's upstairs in our suite. He had some business in this area, so he's joining me for the reunion."

"That's great—I haven't seen Don in a long time," said Grandfather. "Let's go on up." He quickly got the suitcases out of the back of the car. "We're in Suite B-8," he said, leading the way.

"Great—Don and I are right next door, in B-10," Joel said.

The children followed their grandfather and Joel into Suite B-8.

"Oh, look—we can even cook here!" Jessie said when she spotted the kitchen area at the end of the room. It had a small refrigerator and stove, and a small round table.

"Yes, that way we won't have to eat all our meals at the dining hall," said Grandfather.

Off the living room were three smaller rooms, each containing two twin beds.

"One room for the girls, one for the boys, and the third for Grandfather," said Jessie.

"That's right," said Grandfather as they each put their suitcases in their rooms.

"These rooms are nice," said Violet.

"This was where the upperclassmen— the older students—lived," Grandfather explained. "It looks like they've fixed them up a lot since I was here," he added with a chuckle, admiring the new windows and carpeting.

"Look!" Benny said, pointing out the window. "You can see the clock tower from here!" The Aldens looked up the hill and saw the tower at the top, outlined against the darkening sky.

"Come next door," Joel said. "We'll get Don, and then we can all go to dinner together. They're having a special welcome meal in the dining hall."

"Great!" said Benny. "I'm starving."

"You're always starving," said Jessie.

Everyone headed next door. Sitting on the couch in Joel's suite was a large, dark-haired man reading a book. The children knew he had to be Joel's son because he looked so much like him.

"Don!" Joel said. "The Aldens are here."

Don stood up quickly. He looked concerned, but his face quickly brightened when he saw Grandfather. He closed his book and tucked it quickly behind his back. "James Alden, good to see you," he said. He awkwardly transferred the book he'd been holding to his left hand and put out his right to shake Grandfather's.

"It's been too long," Grandfather said.

"I was just, uh…reading," Don said. He looked slightly uncomfortable.

"Still reading that book I got you?" Joel asked his son. He turned to the others. "It's so funny. For years I've been trying to get Don to come visit my old school, and he was never interested. But then I gave him this book, and suddenly he couldn't wait to come!"

Joel laughed his big, friendly laugh. He

went to take the book from his son and show it to the Aldens, but Don didn't seem to want to let go of it. Instead Don held the book up for them to see. Printed on the faded leather cover were the words Goldwin University.

"That book looks really old," said Jessie. "Where did you find it?"

"In an antique store," Joel said. "It's over one hundred years old!"

"Wow!" said Benny. "Can I look at it?"

"I thought we were going to dinner," Don said quickly, putting the book out of reach on a high shelf.

Benny was sorry not to get a look at the book, but he was always ready to eat. "Dinner sounds great!"

***

Goldwin's main dining hall was right next to the clock tower. A large sign over the heavy wooden doors said, Welcome Alumni!

Grandfather looked around as they walked inside. Then he smiled at Joel. "Hasn't changed a bit," he said.

"What are alum—alum—whatever that word is?" asked Benny.

"Alumni are people who graduated from this school," Grandfather explained. "Like Joel and me. Look, Joel—there's where we sign in."

They stopped at a table that was set up by the door and were given a schedule of the week's events and name tags for the whole family.

"Something smells good!" Joel said after he'd put on his name tag.

"Sure does," Benny agreed.

Joel led the way over to the counter and handed everyone a tray. One by one, they all walked down the buffet line, selecting what they wanted to eat. There was pot roast, chicken, potatoes and vegetables, fresh fruit, and Jell-O in all different colors.

When they'd filled their trays, Grandfather noticed an empty table near the windows. "Let's go sit over there."

They had just sat down when an elderly woman walked by holding a tray. As she passed their table, she stopped short and her eyes opened wide. "Well, if it isn't Jimmy Alden!" she said, smiling broadly. The woman was wearing a brightly colored dress, a floppy hat with a large pink flower on it, and bright pink sneakers to match.

Mr. Alden looked at her for a moment before realizing who it was. "Professor Meyer!" he said at last. "My favorite history teacher."

"I hoped my star pupil would remember me," she said, resting her tray on their table. "You know, you can call me Julia now that you're not in my class."

"And I hope you remember me too," said Joel.

"Of course I do—Joel Dixon!" said Professor Meyer. "I rarely saw you and Jimmy apart. I'm so glad to see you're still good friends."

Jessie giggled. "It's funny to hear people call Grandfather 'Jimmy.'"

"So you're Jimmy's grandchildren, are you?" the professor asked her.

"Yes. I'm Jessie, and this is Henry, Benny, and Violet." Jessie motioned to each of her brothers and her sister in turn.

"It sure is nice to meet you," Professor Meyer said, adjusting her hat.

"Professor Meyer knows everything about this college," Grandfather told the children.

"Everything?" Don asked, leaning forward in his chair.

"I probably do," Julia agreed. "After all, I've been here a long time—over fifty years! I always thought I'd leave one day, maybe get a job where I could make a little more money. But that's okay. Now I'm working on—oh, let's just call it my special project— maybe I'll be able to make a little money without ever leaving Goldwin." She smiled and raised her eyebrows as she picked up her tray. "I'm sure I'll see you again this week!"

"It was nice meeting you," Violet said as the professor walked away.

"I wonder what her special project is," said Henry.

"It certainly did sound a little mysterious," Joel said.

"Don't start talking about mysteries with these kids," warned Grandfather. "They are master mystery solvers!"

"Really?" said Don. "I'm a mystery solver too."

"Yes, Don was always playing detective as a kid," Joel agreed.

"Tell us about yours," Don said to the kids.

As they ate, the Aldens told Joel and Don about some of the exciting adventures they'd had, like the time they traveled to England and found the queen's jewels, and the time Jessie joined a hockey team coached by a hockey superstar. Don told them about the mysteries he'd solved when he was young. After they'd all finished eating, they still sat and talked for a long time. Grandfather and Joel Dixon recognized many people walking by who had been their friends years before.

"Grandfather sure did have a lot of friends in college," Benny said.

It was dark when the Aldens and the Dixons finally left the dining hall. As they came out of the building, they saw the clock tower directly in front of them, lit up against the night sky. A golden full moon shone high above the tower.

"Wow, look at that!" said Jessie, her eyes wide. "It looks even cooler at night than during the day."

"It sure does," Henry agreed.

"I wouldn't be surprised if it really was haunted," said Benny. He stared up at the windows of the clock tower. The room at the top looked dark and empty.

"Haunted!" Joel said. "That boy sure has a good imagination, Jim."

"Yes, he does," Grandfather agreed, tousling Benny's hair.

Benny laughed with the others. But as they walked back down the hill, he couldn't help taking one last peek over his shoulder at the moonlit tower.

***

When the Aldens got back to their suite, they were worn out from their long day. In no time they were all asleep.

In the middle of the night, Benny woke up feeling thirsty. He rubbed his eyes and looked at the clock beside his bed. It was midnight. Benny slowly walked to the bathroom and got himself a drink of water.

As he was heading back to bed, Benny walked past the window. He stopped to look at the clock tower standing at the top of the

hill. The full moon was now directly behind it. The clock face was shining brightly, as before, but something had changed. A dim light was glowing in the window at the top of the tower. Benny could see a shadowy figure moving around.

"Oh, my goodness!" Benny said softly to himself. "There's someone up there! But Ezra said no one's up there at night."

Suddenly Benny had another thought. "What if it's the ghost?"

CHAPTER 3

A Ghost in the Tower

Benny rushed over to Henry's bed. "Henry! Henry! Wake up!"

"Who—what—?" Henry said, startled, sitting up quickly in bed, clutching his blankets. "Benny, what's going on?"

"Henry, there's somebody up in the tower! I think it's a ghost!" Benny explained.

"What are you talking about?" Henry asked.

"Come here! Look!" Benny cried, taking Henry by the hand and pulling him over to the window. "See?" He pointed up at the clock tower.

Henry rubbed his sleepy eyes and looked where Benny was pointing. "Yes? So?" he said sleepily.

"Don't you see?" Benny asked. "There's a light on, and it's midnight! Remember what Ezra said? He said nobody goes in the tower at night."

"It certainly *is* strange," Henry agreed. "But it can't be a ghost. I'm sure there's a simple explanation and we'll find out in the morning."

Benny looked out the window again. "But—" he began. "Oh, all right," Benny said, getting slowly into his own bed.

Soon Benny was asleep, but Henry lay awake a little longer. *There couldn't possibly be anything wrong in the clock tower*, he thought. But he wasn't so sure.

***

The next day, the Aldens woke up early, excited about exploring the university. As they walked to the dining hall for breakfast, Benny told the others about what he'd seen the night before.

"It was definitely a ghost," Benny said.

Henry grinned. "Probably not, although it did seem pretty strange that someone would be up there so late at night."

"Well, I'm sure there's a simple explanation," Grandfather assured them.

"That's just what I said," Henry told them.

After a hearty breakfast of juice, milk, and blueberry pancakes with syrup, Grandfather turned to Jessie, who was holding the schedule of reunion activities. "What looks good for this morning?" he asked.

"Let's see," she said, scanning down the page. She read aloud, "'Saturday morning. Take a tour of the campus. See what's changed and what's the same. Meet at the base of the clock tower at ten a.m.'"

"That sounds interesting," said Violet.

Grandfather looked at his watch. "It's quarter to ten now."

"Let's go!" said Henry.

They were just approaching the clock tower when Violet spotted a familiar face. "Isn't that Ezra Stewart?" she asked. They walked over to say hello.

"Hello, Alden family. And what are you doing on this beautiful sunny day?" Ezra asked. He was as sharply dressed as he'd been the day before. Today he wore red-and-white suspenders with the Goldwin insignia on them. The children could guess that he appreciated school spirit.

"We're going on a tour of the campus," Jessie said.

"Doesn't that sound delightful," Ezra commented.

"I have a question for you," Benny said.

Ezra smiled down at Benny. "Fire away! Goldwin University trivia is my specialty."

"Last night, in the middle of the night, I saw a light on in the clock tower," Benny said. "Is someone up there at night?"

The smile on Ezra's face disappeared. "No, of course there isn't anyone up there at night," he said angrily. "Why would you think that?"

Benny seemed hurt by Ezra's tone. "Well, it's just that I saw a light—"

"You must have been mistaken," Ezra snapped. "Maybe you were dreaming."

"I saw it too," Henry pointed out.

Ezra turned to Henry. "Then you must have been mistaken as well," he repeated.

"Is the tower locked at night?" Jessie asked.

"Well, no, I don't lock it, but I told you—nobody goes up there at night," Ezra said. "Now excuse me, but I must be going." He hurried off.

"My goodness, he certainly seemed upset, didn't he?" said Jessie.

"But he was so nice at first," said Benny sadly.

Violet spoke up. "It's like yesterday, when he started talking about his assistant, Andrea Barton. All of a sudden his whole mood changed."

"I guess he didn't like the idea that someone was up there who shouldn't be," Grandfather said.

"But don't you see?" Benny said, suddenly getting excited. "If Ezra says that no one goes up there at night, then there's only one explanation."

"And what might that be?" Jessie asked.

"It's a ghost! I told you!" Benny insisted.

"Oh, Benny," Henry said. "You know there's no such thing as ghosts."

"Are you sure?" Benny asked.

"Yes," said Grandfather. "Maybe Ezra is right, you were mistaken about the light. Maybe it was just a reflection from somewhere else."

"Or maybe someone is going up there who shouldn't be," said Henry.

Before the Aldens could discuss this possibility further, they heard a loud voice. "Good morning, Aldens!"

The family turned to see Joel and Don Dixon coming up the hill to join them. "Ready for the tour?"

"We sure are," said Grandfather.

Just then a blond man in a red Goldwin University T-shirt called out, "The tour is going to be starting now." The Dixons and Aldens walked toward him. A small group of people gathered around. "My name is Ethan, and I'll be your guide," the man said. "Some of the buildings you may remember, but a lot have been built since you graduated. You'll see they're working on a brand-new building right here on the Quad." He motioned behind him. "I'm sure you all remember the clock tower."

People nodded and smiled. "Hasn't changed a bit," one woman pointed out.

"When was the tower built?" asked Don.

"Around 1860. It's one of the oldest buildings here," Ethan said.

"Did it always have a carillon?" Don asked.

"Yes," said Ethan. "At the beginning, there were twenty-five bells. Over the years, more and more bells were donated to the school by generous alumni. Now there are forty-nine.

"We'll end our tour back here in time for the midday concert," Ethan continued. "Now, if you'll follow me, let's head on over this way, to the new science buildings."

"How old is the clock?" Don asked.

Ethan turned around. "You have a lot of good questions," he remarked. "It's the original clock—from 1860," Ethan said.

Don nodded.

"If there are no more questions, we'll move on," Ethan said, looking around at the group.

Joel and Grandfather were very impressed with the new science buildings, which were very tall and faced with glass. "They look a lot fancier than the old labs we had our classes in," Joel remarked. "Very modern buildings, don't you think, Don?"

Don seemed lost in his own thoughts.

"Don?" Joel asked after a moment.

"I'm sorry, Dad. What did you say?" asked Don.

"I was just noticing how modern these buildings are compared to the rest of the campus," said Joel.

"What? Oh, yes," Don said. But he didn't really seem to be paying attention.

A moment later, Ethan had led the tour to a group of very old-looking dormitories. "A Civil War battle was fought not far from here, and troops were housed in some of these buildings."

"What's the Civil War?" asked Benny.

"That was a war fought between the northern and southern parts of our country," said Grandfather. "It happened a long time ago, in the 1860s."

"Really? There was a war in the United States?" asked Benny.

"Yes, and lots of young men and boys left their families to go and fight," Grandfather said. "Many people were killed, or lost their homes and all their money. It was a terrible war."

The tour continued past many more interesting buildings and a large statue of James Goldwin, founder of the college. Finally they found themselves back at the clock tower.

"We'll go up to the top of the tower now, for anyone who wants to see the view," Ethan said.

"Great," said several people in the crowd as they headed into the tower and started up the steep, winding staircase. The Aldens followed, even though they'd already seen the view the day before. Ethan pointed out several more sights from the top of the tower. When he was finished, he said, "And that concludes our tour. Thanks so much for joining me."

"Thank you," said Jessie, and others on the tour echoed her.

The Aldens waited as the rest of the group

headed back down the stairs. Just as they were getting ready to leave, a young woman came hurrying up the stairs. She was wearing blue jeans, clogs, and a bulky red sweatshirt with the word GOLDWIN stitched across the front in large white letters. Her long brown hair was pulled back in a ponytail that bounced as she walked.

"Hello!" Benny said as she entered the tower room. "You missed the tour, but I can tell you what we saw."

"Thanks," the woman said with a big smile, "but I go to school here. I probably could have given the tour."

"I bet you don't know all the stuff about the carillon," Benny said.

"I bet I do," the woman said, her smile growing larger. "I'm the assistant carillon player."

"You are?" Violet said. She remembered how upset Ezra had been when he talked about his assistant. This young woman seemed nice and friendly. How could she make him so angry?

"You must be Andrea Barton," Henry said.

"That's right. But you can call me Andi— all my friends do. How did you know my name?" Andrea asked.

"We met Ezra yesterday," Jessie said. "He told us all about the carillon, and we watched him play a concert."

"Pretty cool, isn't it?" Andrea said. "I'm giving the concert at noon. I came a little early to get ready." She looked around at the stacks of papers everywhere. She lifted a few piles and frowned.

"What are you looking for?" asked Henry.

"My glasses," Andi said. "I'm sure I left them here. And the other day I bought some new pieces of music to try out, and they disappeared too. Then again, I'm not sure Ezra liked the idea of new music anyway." Andi opened a few drawers in the desk and looked inside. "It's almost as if there's a ghost in here, moving my things around!"

Benny's face lit up. "See? I told you there was a ghost," he said to his brother and sisters.

Andi laughed.

"Here are some glasses," Jessie said, picking up a pair that was lying on the windowsill.

She handed them to Andi.

"Those aren't mine," Andi said. "They look like they belong to someone older. See, they have a little line in the middle of the glass. That means they're bifocals."

"Like mine," Grandfather said, taking off his glasses and cleaning them with his handkerchief. "The top part helps you see far away, and the bottom part helps you see close up."

"Maybe they belong to Ezra," Violet suggested.

"No," Andi said. "He doesn't wear glasses."

"Maybe someone on the tour left them," Jessie suggested.

"I don't remember anyone wearing glasses," said Henry.

"I bet they belong to the ghost!" said Benny.

"Benny thinks the clock tower is haunted," Henry explained. "He saw a light moving around up here late last night."

"Late last night?" Andi repeated. Then she laughed quickly. "Who would be up here in the middle of the night?"

"That's just what we were wondering,"

Jessie said. "We asked Ezra, and he said no one is supposed to be in here after the evening concert."

"That's right. I come up in between concerts a lot to practice," Andi said. "But not in the middle of the night, of course." She laughed again, a little nervously.

"That's why I think it's a ghost. A ghost who doesn't see very well, I guess." Benny waved the glasses.

"I guess not." Andi grinned at Benny. Then her face grew serious again, and she began shuffling through the papers some more. "And now I really do have to get ready for my concert."

"We'll go downstairs and listen from the Quad," Grandfather suggested. He had noticed that Andi seemed nervous. "I'm sure it's not easy to play with all of us standing right here."

Back down on the ground, the Aldens bought sandwiches and drinks at a small lunch stand set up next to the Quad. As they ate their picnic lunch, they listened to Andi's concert.

"I guess she found her music," Jessie said.

"Her music is a lot jazzier than Ezra's was," said Violet.

"Hey, I know this song," Henry pointed out. "It's a pop song. I heard it on the radio yesterday as we were driving."

"That's neat that she can play it on the carillon," Violet said.

"Ezra's stuff was good too, but it was more classical music," Jessie remarked.

When the concert ended, Violet turned to the others. "She's a really great player. I wonder why she was so nervous."

"She was probably just excited about her concert," Jessie assured her sister. But privately she wondered whether something was bothering Andi, and whether it had anything to do with the light Benny had seen up in the tower.

CHAPTER 4

Do Ghosts Wear Sneakers?

That night, Henry and Benny were getting ready for bed. They both had their pajamas on and their teeth brushed. They were just climbing into their beds when Benny suddenly jumped back out.

"What are you doing?" Henry asked.

"Getting this," Benny explained, pulling his little alarm clock out of his suitcase.

"You don't need that," Henry said. "Grandfather told us we could sleep in tomorrow morning."

"It's not for tomorrow morning," Benny said. "I'm setting it for midnight so I can see if the ghost is in the clock tower again."

"Benny!" Henry cried, throwing a pillow at his little brother. "Oh...all right."

But a few hours later, Henry wished he'd never agreed. A bell was ringing in his ears, and there was no sign of Benny turning it off.

"Benny! Benny!" Henry called out. "Turn off the alarm!" At last Henry sat up and looked over at Benny's bed. Benny was snuggled down under his covers, sound asleep.

"Oh, sure, you're going to get up," Henry muttered as he reached over to turn off the alarm. He had forgotten what a sound sleeper Benny was. Benny hadn't even heard the alarm.

But Henry had to smile, remembering how excited Benny had been to find out if the "ghost" would be back at midnight. "I won't even wake him," Henry said softly to himself. "I'll just take a quick look and then go back to sleep. I'm sure there's no one up there tonight."

Henry turned to the window. It was raining out. There was the clock tower, the clock shining brightly. And the window of the tower room was dark, just as it should be. Or was it?

Henry took a step closer to the window. He thought he'd seen something. But he must be imagining things. No—there it was again. A small light was flickering in the window.

"What is that?" Henry muttered to himself. He stepped right up to the window and watched as the light bounced around in the tower room. Then he rushed back over to Benny's bed and began shaking him.

"Benny, Benny! Wake up!" Henry cried.

It took Benny a few seconds to wake up and figure out where he was. "Henry?" he asked, rubbing his eyes. "What's going on?"

"Benny, hurry up! Come look!" Henry cried, pulling Benny to his feet. "There's a light in the tower!"

"There is?" Benny asked. He ran to the window and the two boys stood side by side in the dark room, looking up at the tower.

"Wow!" Benny said. "Someone's up there."

"But I don't think it's the same person as last night," Henry said.

"How do you know?" Benny asked.

"Because last night, the whole room was lit," Henry explained. "But tonight, it's just a little light bouncing around—like someone's carrying a flashlight."

"You're right!" Benny said. "Let's go wake the others."

A moment later, Jessie and Violet were standing beside their brothers looking up at the tower.

"Why would someone be up there with a flashlight on?" Jessie asked. "Why not just turn on the light?"

"I don't know," said Henry. "Unless this person doesn't want anyone to know he—or she—is there."

After several minutes, the light went out. The Aldens waited a few more minutes before agreeing that whoever had been up there must have left.

"Can we go back to sleep now?" Violet asked, yawning.

"Yes, definitely," said Henry.

"But what about our ghost?" Benny asked.

"First of all, it's *not* a ghost," Jessie said.

"How do you know?" Benny demanded.

"Well, aside from the fact that there's no such thing as ghosts, a ghost certainly wouldn't need to carry a flashlight," Jessie pointed out.

"Yeah, I guess you're right," Benny said. He sounded disappointed. "So who is it, then?"

"I don't know," said Jessie. Then she yawned. "But I'm tired. We'll figure it out in the morning."

***

The next morning the Aldens were awakened by the sound of the bells playing outside. But something was wrong.

"The song sounds awful!" Violet said.

"I wonder what's wrong," Jessie said.

A moment later the music stopped, right in the middle. There was a strange, sudden silence. Jessie and Violet quickly got dressed and joined their brothers in the small kitchenette.

"What happened to the bells?" Benny asked.

"I don't know," said Jessie. "The song sounded all wrong."

The children made some breakfast with

the groceries they'd bought the day before—scrambled eggs, toast and jam, orange juice, and a cup of coffee for Grandfather. Just as everything was ready, Grandfather came out of the bathroom, freshly showered and shaved.

"Something smells good," Grandfather said.

"We made breakfast," Jessie said. "Come and have some."

As the Aldens sat down to eat, they told Grandfather about the carillon. He hadn't heard it because he'd been in the shower.

"It sounded fine last night," Grandfather said.

"Maybe whoever was up there last night did something to it," Benny said.

"Someone was up there last night?" Mr. Alden asked.

The children told him what they'd seen at midnight.

"I think we should go up there this morning and investigate," said Benny.

"You go ahead," said Grandfather. "I'll just relax with my coffee and read the paper. But be back here by noon. There's a picnic this afternoon that should be a lot of fun."

"Okay, Grandfather," Jessie called as they left.

Half an hour later, the Aldens were climbing the hill to the tower.

"It sure is muddy," Violet pointed out.

"It rained pretty hard last night," Henry said. "Be careful you don't slip."

When they got up to the tower room, Ezra was there, a toolbox in his hands. He was not in a good mood. "Did you hear the bells this morning?" he asked when he saw the Aldens.

"Yes," said Violet. "What happened to them?"

Ezra shook his head. "I'm not sure, but the whole carillon is a mess. Somehow, several of the wires and springs were broken, and some of the clappers were loosened. Look." The children looked where Ezra was pointing. Just as he had said, several wires seemed to have been snapped, so they no longer went all the way down into the carillon.

"When I tried to play my usual morning piece, several bells weren't ringing when they were supposed to," said Ezra. "When I realized what was happening, I stopped and went to get my toolbox. I've been trying to fix the carillon and the bells ever since."

"This couldn't have just happened by accident, could it?" Henry asked.

"I bet it has something to do with the person who was up here last night," said Benny.

Ezra stopped what he was doing and looked up. "What person?"

"We don't exactly know," said Benny.

"What Benny means is, we saw a light up here last night," Jessie explained.

"We think someone was in here, carrying a flashlight," added Henry.

"Maybe that person broke the bells," Benny said.

"You saw a light?" Ezra said.

"Yes," said Benny.

Ezra frowned for a moment. "Did you see anything else besides the light?"

"No," said Jessie.

"Listen," Ezra said gruffly. "I get up very early to do the morning concert. I come up with my coffee and my paper before the sun's even up. Now, if you'll excuse me, I've got to go back to my house—my small screwdriver isn't in here. I must have left it at home. I'll be back in a little while."

Ezra had just left when suddenly Violet spotted something.

On the floor beside the practice carillon was a muddy footprint. Violet turned to Benny. "Do ghosts wear sneakers?" she asked, pointing.

"Hey! Look at that!" Henry cried. Jessie hurried over to look at the footprint.

"This wasn't here yesterday, was it?" Jessie asked.

"No—we would have noticed it," said Violet.

"And it just started raining last night, so there wasn't any mud yesterday," said Henry. "Whoever left this must have been here since last night."

"It probably wasn't Ezra," said Henry. "He wears loafers, and they have smooth soles."

"What kind of shoes does Andi wear?" Benny asked.

"When we met her she had on clogs," said

Violet. "I remember because I thought they looked so comfortable."

"Do you think the person who left this print is the same person who broke the carillon?" Jessie asked.

"I don't know," said Henry. "It could be."

"And don't forget those glasses we found," said Violet. "Someone left those up here too."

"I knew we'd get another mystery to solve!" said Benny. And he broke into a big grin.

CHAPTER 5

Buried Treasure!

The Aldens headed back to their dormitory, still talking about the footprint.

The Aldens' suite was empty, but the children heard voices from next door. They knocked on the Dixons' suite and found Grandfather and Joel sitting in the living room, drinking coffee and chatting.

"Come join us," Grandfather said.

"Have a doughnut," Joel offered, motioning to the box on the small kitchen table.

"Thanks," said Jessie as she and the others

each took a powdery sugar doughnut.

The two men went back to their conversation as the children sat down at the kitchen table and ate.

"Look, here's Don's old book about Goldwin," Violet said, spotting the book with the cracked leather cover lying on the kitchen counter.

"I bet it has some neat old pictures," said Jessie. "Joel, is it okay if we look at Don's book?"

"Sure," Joel replied.

As Benny reached for the book, Jessie quickly added, "First we need to wash our hands."

The children washed the powdered sugar off their fingers and dried their hands carefully. Then Violet picked up the book and put it in the center of the table. Everyone gathered around as she turned the pages one by one.

"Look at this old picture of the campus," said Henry, pointing to a brown-tinted photograph. "There are only a few buildings here."

"And here's one that shows them building the clock tower," said Benny.

"Wow," said Jessie. "It says underneath that from the top of the tower you can see all the way to Buttermilk Falls. We'll have to look for that next time we're up there."

"Hey, look, there's a chapter called 'The Secrets of Goldwin University,'" said Henry.

"Secrets?" said Benny. "What secrets?"

Henry began to read a little bit of the chapter. "It says there are many secret hidden places on campus. And there are rumors of a treasure buried here!"

"A treasure!" the others repeated.

"I'd like to see that," said Benny.

Just then the door opened and Don came in. "Hello," he called out.

"Have a nice walk?" Joel asked him.

"Sure did," said Don. "I walked by the river, all the way up to the waterfalls and back."

"We were just having some coffee and doughnuts," said Mr. Alden. "Come join us."

"Don't mind if I do," said Don, going into the kitchen area to get himself some coffee. "What have you kids been up to?"

"Not much," said Jessie. "We were just looking at this old book of yours. I hope you don't mind."

"No, not at all," said Don, pouring himself a cup of coffee. Suddenly he turned around. "Wait a minute—what book?"

"This one," said Violet, holding it up. "The one about Goldwin."

Don put down his coffee cup and grabbed the book out of Violet's hands. "Where did you find this?" he demanded.

"It was right here in the kitchen," Henry said.

"We were being really careful with it," said Jessie. "We made sure our hands were clean."

Don turned a few pages, as if making sure the book was still in one piece. "This is a very old, delicate book," he said angrily. "It's not something to play with."

"But we weren't playing—" said Benny. But it was too late. Don had taken the book and strode quickly out of the room. A moment later he was back, empty-handed. "I'm sorry, but that book is very...special to me. I wouldn't want anything to happen to it." He

picked up his coffee cup and walked into the living room to sit down with the two men.

The children just looked at one another quietly, wondering about Don's sudden anger. Why would he get so upset over a book?

A short while later, it was time to go to the picnic. It was being held on the Quad, and there were tables and tables piled with food: fried chicken, all different kinds of salads, rolls, pickles, and watermelon and cupcakes for dessert. The Aldens and the Dixons each helped themselves to a plateful of food and then sat down in the shade to enjoy it. When he'd finished his first plateful, Benny went back two more times to get more of the delicious potato salad and extra slices of watermelon.

At the end of the lively afternoon, the Aldens walked into town and had dinner at the Chariot, one of Grandfather's favorite pizza places. "We used to come here all the time when I was a student," he told them.

"I can't believe it's still here," said Jessie.

"Wait till you taste the pizza. Then you'll believe it," Mr. Alden assured her.

The pizza was just as good as Grandfather had promised. After dinner, the Aldens took a stroll through town. Grandfather couldn't believe all the large buildings that had been built since he was there last.

When they finally returned to their suite, the children were worn out.

"I'm ready for bed," said Benny. "I'm not even going to set the alarm tonight."

"Good!" said Henry. "I could use a good night's sleep."

***

The next morning, the Aldens awoke feeling rested and ready for another busy day of activities.

"There's a concert this afternoon that Joel and I are going to," said Grandfather, "but I think I'm just going to relax in the room this morning. What do you kids plan to do?"

"I want to look for the treasure," said Benny.

"Treasure?" asked Grandfather.

Jessie told him what they'd read the day before in Don's book.

"I was here for four years and I never saw

any treasure," Mr. Alden said with a chuckle. "But enjoy yourselves. Meet me back here for lunch."

"Remember the book also said that from the top of the clock tower you can see all the way to the waterfalls," said Jessie.

"That's right," Violet recalled. "Let's go up and see if you really can. It's a clear day."

Once again, the Aldens found themselves climbing to the top of the tower. "Our leg muscles are getting a good workout here," said Henry.

"They sure are," Violet agreed.

The top of the tower was dark and quiet today. The morning concert had ended a short while ago, and no one was up there.

"Now, what did it say in the book?" Henry asked.

"If you look out the west window you can see Buttermilk Falls," Jessie reminded him.

"How do we know which window faces west?" asked Benny.

"The sun came up over there," said Violet. "So that's the east."

"Then that's the west," Jessie said, pointing

to the opposite window.

The children all went to that window and looked out.

"Look, there are the falls!" Henry said, pointing off in the distance.

"I see people climbing on the rocks," Jessie said.

"Hey, let me see," said Benny.

Jessie moved aside to give Benny room to look out. As she turned away from the window, she noticed a folded piece of paper on the floor in the corner. "What's that?" she mumbled to herself. She went over and picked up the piece of paper. It was yellowed and felt strange—crumbly and rough, as if it were very old. Jessie carefully unfolded the paper and was surprised by the fancy writing on it.

"You guys!" she said. "Look at this!"

The other children turned around to see what Jessie was holding.

"What have you got?" Violet asked.

"A letter," Jessie said. "Only it's really old. I found it in the corner."

The others crowded around.

"There's a seal at the top," Henry said, pointing to a circle design that had been pressed into the top of the paper. "It says, 'Goldwin University, Office of the President.'"

"What does that mean?" asked Benny. "Is this from the president of the United States?"

"No, it's from the president of this college," Jessie explained. "The president at a university is sort of like the principal at your school. This is his or her stationery."

"It says 'May 5, 1863' in the corner," Violet pointed out. "This letter is really old—it was written over a hundred years ago!"

"Wow!" said Benny.

"That's even older than Grandfather," Violet pointed out.

"So what does it say?" Benny asked. "The writing looks really strange."

"They didn't have ballpoint pens back then," Jessie said. "They had to dip their pens in ink to write. And people had very fancy handwriting."

"They sure did," said Benny. "I can't even read it." He had just learned to read and had enough trouble with regular printing.

"This is what it says," said Jessie, reading aloud:

Dear Aaron,
I have hidden our gold and silver so the army shall not get it. Do not be concerned— it shall be safe until you come home from the war, and only then shall we dig it up. Should anything happen to me, I give you this clue to where it lies hidden:
Listen to the music and take one hundred sixty-one steps. Remember, the key to the problem is right before the face.
Your loving father

When Jessie had finished reading, she looked up to see her sister and two brothers all standing openmouthed, staring at her.

"I don't believe it!" said Violet.

"There really is a treasure buried here!" said Henry.

"I knew it! I knew it!" said Benny.

"Wait a minute," Jessie said. "Let's think about this before we go and get all excited. We don't even know if this letter is real!"

"It looks real," said Benny.

"It certainly does," Violet had to agree, fingering the embossed seal of the president's office. "I mean, look at this crumbling old paper. And people just don't write like this anymore."

"But where did the letter come from?" asked Henry. "We've been up here several times in the last few days, and this is the first time we've seen it."

"You're right," Violet agreed. "Someone must have just dropped this here recently."

"Do you think the person who dropped it was hunting for the treasure?" Benny asked.

"Could be," said Henry.

"What do you think we should do, Jessie?" Violet asked.

Jessie had been silently staring out the window. Suddenly she turned around. "I know how we can find out if this letter is real."

"How?" asked Violet.

"The library is right down there." Jessie pointed out the window. "Let's go there and look up some information about the history of Goldwin University."

"Great idea," Henry said.

Jessie folded the letter carefully and the four children hurried down the narrow staircase, going as quickly as they could on the twisting stone steps.

A few minutes later, the Aldens were at the front desk of Goldwin's main library. The librarian there was tall and thin with short brown hair. "Hello, I'm Mrs. Brooke. Can I help you?" she asked.

"We're looking for a book that has information about the history of the college," said Jessie.

"Just a minute," Mrs. Brooke said. She came back a moment later with a thick, heavy book. The cover read, *Goldwin University: From Past to Present.* "This book has a lot of information."

"Thanks," said Henry, picking up the large book and walking over to a table by a window. The others followed. He set the book down and opened it to the table of contents. The children studied the page for a moment.

"This sounds like a good place to look," Henry said, pointing to a chapter titled

"Presidents of the University." "It starts on page fifty-six."

Jessie flipped to that page. She read aloud from the first page, "'The university was founded in 1860 and the first president was named Joshua Chambers. He held the office until 1864.'"

"This letter was written in 1863," said Violet. "So he must be the one who wrote it."

"Look, there's a picture," Benny pointed out. "Is that him?"

Jessie looked at the black-and-white picture of a handsome man with dark hair and small round glasses. Underneath the photograph it said, *Joshua Chambers, First President of Goldwin University.* "Yes, Benny, that's him."

The children studied the photograph for a moment.

"Let's see what else it says about him," Jessie suggested. She quickly read the page to herself. Suddenly her eyes widened and she gasped.

"What is it?" Benny asked. "Tell us!"

"He's the one who wrote the letter," said Jessie.

"How do you know?" Henry asked.

"It says that he had a son named Aaron who served in the army during the Civil War," Jessie told them.

"And this letter is addressed to someone named Aaron, from his father," said Violet.

Jessie continued reading. Suddenly she said, "Oh, how terrible!"

"What?" the other three cried.

Jessie explained, "It says that Chambers died in 1864, while his son was off at war— and Aaron was killed in battle a few months later."

"How sad," Violet said.

"He died the year after he wrote the letter," Benny said.

The children were silent for a moment. They gazed at the picture of the kind-looking man and thought about how sad his story was.

All of a sudden Henry said, "Do you realize what this means? President Chambers died before he got to show his son where the treasure was."

"But remember, there were some clues in the letter," Benny said.

"I wonder if Aaron figured them out," Violet said.

"He might not have had a chance," said Henry. "It says he was killed in a battle just a short time after his father died."

"Then that means..." Jessie began.

"The treasure is still buried!" Benny whispered.

CHAPTER 6

Going on a Treasure Hunt

"Now, just wait a minute, Benny," Henry said. "Someone might already have found the treasure, you know. I mean, we're not the first ones to have seen this letter."

"No, we're not," Jessie agreed. "I wonder who found it first and who left it in the tower."

"Even if we're not the first, we can still look for the treasure, can't we?" Benny asked.

"Yes, we certainly can," said Henry.

"Let's take a look at what it says in the letter again," suggested Jessie. "But first I'm going to return this book to Mrs. Brooke."

While Jessie took the book back to the librarian, Violet laid the letter on top of the table and carefully unfolded it.

"What does the clue say again?" Benny asked.

Violet read, "It says, 'Listen to the music and take one hundred sixty-one steps. Remember, the key to the problem is right in front of the face.'"

"What do you think he meant by 'listen to the music'?" asked Jessie, who had just come back.

"They definitely didn't have radios or CDs back then," said Henry with a laugh.

As they were talking, the silence of the library was broken by the sound of the bells.

"The midday concert!" Violet cried.

"I know, can you believe it's already lunchtime?" Jessie asked.

"And it sounds like Ezra fixed the carillon," Henry added.

"No, I mean, that's the music you listen to here at Goldwin," Violet said excitedly. "The music Joshua Chambers was talking about!"

"You're right!" Jessie said. "Good thinking, Violet."

"Did the carillon play way back then?" Henry asked.

"Yes," Jessie said. "On the tour they said it was put in when the tower was first built. That was in 1860."

"Okay, so we've figured out the first part of the clue," said Henry. "Now what about the rest of it?"

"Read the second part again," Benny said.

Violet read, " 'Take one hundred sixty-one steps—' "

"I know!" Benny shouted all of a sudden. "That's how many steps it is to the top of the clock tower. Remember, Mr. Stewart told us that the first day we met him?"

"Great job, Benny!" said Jessie.

"You have a good memory," Henry added.

"So President Chambers was telling his son to go to the top of the tower," Violet said.

"Then why are we still sitting here?" Benny asked. "Let's go!"

The children hurried out of the library and walked as quickly as they could up the winding tower stairs.

At the top, they found Ezra playing the carillon. He gave the children a smile as they came in. He seemed to have fixed all the broken wires. The children looked around the room, wondering where the treasure might be hidden.

When Ezra had finished playing, he turned to the children. "What brings you all back here again?"

"We're on a treasure hunt!" Benny said.

"A treasure hunt?" Ezra repeated. "Oh, I see. Why are you looking up here? Nothing here but a bunch of old music books. And the carillon, of course."

"I see you've fixed it," Henry said.

"Yes, I did," Ezra said. "It took me all morning. But I think it sounds okay now."

"It sounded good to me," said Violet.

Jessie showed Ezra the old letter. "This is why we're on a treasure hunt," she explained. "We found this up here after you left."

Ezra took the letter Jessie was holding. "This looks very old! Wherever did you find it?"

"Right here, in the corner," Benny said.

"I wonder how it got there," Ezra said. He read the letter and handed it back to Violet. "I can't believe I wouldn't notice something like this."

"We figured out that the letter was from President Joshua Chambers," Jessie said. "And it seems he was telling his son to come up here to the clock tower."

"Well, as I said, there's no treasure up here. I've been here long enough to know that." Ezra went over to his desk and put away the music he'd just played.

Jessie took another look at the letter. "What do you think he means by the 'key to the problem'?"

The children all thought about that for a moment. They looked around at the old photos on the walls.

Just then the bells played four loud notes, startling the children.

"What was that?" asked Benny.

"That means it's quarter to one," Ezra said. "The bells are programmed to ring the hours, quarter hours, and half hours by themselves.

The bells aren't just for music; they also work with the clock."

All of a sudden Henry said, "Hey! Maybe that's it."

"What's it?" asked Jessie

"I have an idea about what Chambers meant when he said the answer is 'right before the face,'" Henry said. "Look up there!" He pointed to a large round door over the west-facing window. "That's the back of the clock, right, Ezra?"

"Yes, it is," Ezra said. "I open that door to fix the clock or reset it."

"Think about what you call the front of a clock," Henry said.

"You mean its face?" Jessie asked. Then her face lit up. "Oh, I get it!"

"Maybe President Chambers wasn't talking about a person's face," Henry explained to the others. "Maybe he was talking about the clock's face."

"You mean that somehow the 'key' is in the clock's face?" Benny asked.

"I guess so," Henry said.

"Ezra, is that possible?" asked Jessie.

"Could there be something hidden in the clock's face?"

"I don't see how," Ezra said. "I clean that clock once a month. I'd see anything hidden there."

"Yes, you would," Henry agreed.

"Could you open up the clock now?" Jessie asked. "Maybe there's something in there you never noticed."

"I love to show people how that big old clock works. It's pretty amazing," Ezra said. He went to a cabinet on the wall and took out a small key. Then he pulled a stepladder out from under his desk and placed it under the clock. He got up on the ladder and unlocked the back of the clock. The large round door swung open, revealing the inside of the giant clock.

"Wow, look at that," Benny said, staring at all the gears turning inside the clock. "That's cool."

Ezra gave a quick explanation of how the old clock worked and how he took care of it. "If each of you would like to come up, one at a time, you can take a closer look."

The children took turns stepping up on the ladder and studying the inside of the clock—first Benny, then Violet, then Jessie, and finally Henry.

"Could something have been hidden inside the back here?" Henry asked when it was his turn.

"I can't imagine—I'm sure I'd have seen it by now," Ezra said. "I have to take apart all the machinery to clean it."

"I was so sure there would be something in the clock," Henry said. He was disappointed.

"Can I look again?" Benny asked. He didn't want to give up the treasure hunt yet.

"Go ahead," Ezra said. "But I'm *sure* there's nothing hidden in there."

Henry stepped down from the ladder and Benny stepped back up. He looked all around the clock, trying to think of a place Ezra might never have looked. He noticed a tiny crevice around the rim of the clock, where it attached to the wall. Benny slipped his small fingers in there and felt around. "Hey! There's something in here!" he cried suddenly.

"There is?" Ezra asked.

"Yes, it feels like a little lump of crumbly stuff—paper, maybe," Benny said. "I just can't quite get my fingers around it."

"Maybe there's something in my toolbox that will help," Ezra said.

"I'll look," Jessie offered, going to get Ezra's toolbox from his desk. After a moment she said, "How about these needle-nose pliers?"

"That ought to work," Ezra said. Jessie handed them to him.

Ezra stepped up next to Benny. He poked the long, thin pliers down into the crevice where Benny had felt something. "I've got it—whatever it is," he said. Slowly, he pulled out a small bundle of crumbling brown paper.

"It's a little package," Benny said. "And it looks really old."

Ezra handed the package to Henry as Benny stepped back down the ladder. Ezra closed and locked the clock door. Then he joined the Aldens, who were clustered around his desk. Henry was carefully opening the flat brown package.

"There's a key," he said.

"The 'key to the problem,'" Jessie said with a smile.

"And a note," Henry added. He slowly unwrapped the note and read it aloud.

Aaron—

If you have found this key, then you must have figured out my first note. Good work.

On a warm summer's morn when the clock strikes six, set yourself between North and South. The tower will point the way.

Your father

"Another clue!" Benny said.

"I wonder what it means," Violet said.

"I can't believe it!" Ezra said. "Well, this has certainly been excitement enough for one morning. I'm ready to go home and have my lunch."

"Lunch—that's right," Jessie said. "We were supposed to meet Grandfather back at the suite at lunchtime, remember?"

"May we take this key and note with us, Ezra?" Henry asked.

Ezra paused. "Well, you did find them," he said, "so I guess that would only be fair."

"We'd better go, then," Jessie said. "Thanks for opening the clock for us!"

"My pleasure," Ezra said.

"We'll see you later!" Benny called over his shoulder as he and the other Aldens hurried down the stairs.

***

Back at the suite, Grandfather was just putting his plate and cup in the sink. "Here you are!" he said. "I thought you weren't coming. I went ahead and ate without you."

"Sorry we're so late—" Jessie began.

"But wait until you hear about our treasure hunt!" Benny cut in excitedly.

The Aldens told their grandfather all about what they'd found. When at last they'd finished their story, Grandfather sat looking at the two old letters and the key. "That's amazing!" he said. "So there really is a treasure buried here."

"But how do we find it?" Violet asked.

"I don't know, but I'm sure you will," Grandfather said.

"Can we eat first?" Benny asked. "I'm starving."

"It is way past lunchtime," Jessie said. "It's nearly two o'clock."

"Is it that late?" Grandfather asked. "I'm joining Joel for a concert. It starts at two. I told him I'd meet him in Rhodes Hall, where they're giving the concert. I'd better get going. How about if we meet back here at dinnertime?"

"Sounds great!" Jessie said.

"Be careful with those letters," Grandfather said. "If they're really that old, they're valuable historical documents."

"We'll be very careful," Violet assured him.

"There's ham and cheese in the refrigerator," Grandfather reminded them. "And there's fruit too. See you later!"

The children waved as Grandfather left. Then they made themselves lunch. They had been so busy treasure hunting, they hadn't realized how hungry they were.

After a few minutes Jessie said, "I've been wondering how that letter got into the tower in the first place."

"Me too," said Violet.

"I think someone must have found it—somewhere—and figured out that it was talking about the clock tower, just like we did," said Henry.

"Then that person must have gone up to the tower to look, just like we did. And dropped the note while he or she was there," said Jessie.

"I bet it's the same person who was up there at night," said Violet, selecting a peach from the basket on the counter. "The person went up when he or she knew no one would be around."

"But why?" Benny asked, biting into a plum.

"Probably to keep the treasure and not share it," Jessie said. "But that would be wrong—the treasure belongs to the Chambers family."

"Let's take a look at that second note," Henry said.

As the other children cleared away the lunch dishes, Violet went to get the letters and key. She had placed them on the counter away from the food so they wouldn't get dirty.

When the table was cleared, Violet spread out the second letter. The children sat down to look at it.

"What's a 'morn'?" asked Benny.

"It means morning," Jessie explained. "What do you think he means by 'set yourself between North and South'?"

"I have no idea," said Henry. "It sounds as if he's talking about the Civil War again. That war pitted the North against the South."

"But what does that have to do with the treasure?" Benny wanted to know.

"How do you think the tower will point the way?" Violet asked. "It points straight up in the air."

The children all sat quietly for several minutes.

"I think we need help," Jessie said.

"Who could help us?" Henry wondered. "This time it's not as simple as going to the library."

"Remember Grandfather said Professor Meyer knew everything about Goldwin?" Violet recalled. "Maybe she could help us."

"That's a good idea," Henry said. "She

must have an office here on campus. Let's go find it."

"I bet it's in McGraw Hall," said Jessie. "On our tour they said that was where the history classes were, and Professor Meyer is a history professor."

The Aldens left their suite and headed up the hill to McGraw Hall. As they were cutting across the Quad, they saw Don Dixon heading toward them.

"Hi, Don!" Benny called out.

Don looked up, startled. He seemed lost in his own thoughts and very upset. "Oh, hello," he said distractedly.

"Is something the matter?" Violet asked.

"Something the matter? No, no," Don said. Then he paused. "Do you remember the other day when you were looking through that old book?"

"Yes," Jessie said.

"By any chance, did you notice..." Don stopped talking, and seemed to change his mind. "Oh, never mind."

"Are you sure—" Violet began, but Don cut her off.

"I've got to go." He rushed off down the hill.

The Aldens watched him walk away.

Jessie shrugged. "I wonder what's bugging him."

"Who knows?" said Henry.

"Come on, let's go find Professor Meyer," Benny reminded them.

CHAPTER 7

Guess Who's Coming to Dinner!

A few minutes later, the children were standing inside McGraw Hall, looking up at the directory on the wall.

"It says Professor Meyer's office is on the first floor," said Henry. "Room 106."

The children passed a large lecture hall and found Room 106 at the back of the building. Jessie knocked on the door.

"Come in," said a voice from inside.

Jessie opened the door and stepped in. Professor Meyer was standing next to a large, messy desk covered with papers. She was stuffing some of the papers into a large canvas bag that was already overflowing with papers and books. Again she was wearing a lively patterned dress with a brightly colored hat and matching sneakers.

"Well, if it isn't the Aldens," she said.

"Professor, we have a question for you," said Jessie.

"I hope it's a quick one," Professor Meyer said. "I was just on my way out."

"Actually, it's not a quick one," Jessie said. "Is there another time we could talk to you?"

"How about over dinner?" Henry suggested. "I'm sure our grandfather would enjoy chatting with you as well."

"What a lovely idea," the professor said. "I would invite you to my place, but I'm not much of a cook, I must confess. And my house is such a mess."

Looking around the cluttered office, the children had no trouble believing that.

"We'll make dinner for you at our suite," Jessie offered.

"Now that would be a treat," Professor

Meyer said. "What time shall I come?"

"What time did Grandfather say he'd be home?" Henry asked.

"I think the concert ends at five," Jessie said. "How about six o'clock? We're in Sage Hall, Suite B-8."

"I will see you then," the professor said, picking up her overstuffed bag and putting it on her shoulder. The children stepped into the hallway with her. She shut and locked her office door.

"Where are you going now?" Benny piped up.

"Now? Oh, I'm going to, um…now, where *am* I going?" She paused for a moment. "Where did you say your grandfather was?"

"He's at a concert in Rhodes Hall," said Henry.

"Oh, yes, that's right. That's where I'm headed too," Julia Meyer said.

"You know it started a while ago," Jessie said.

"Did it?" asked Ms. Meyer. "That's all right. I'll just be a little late. Good-bye!"

The children watched her walk away.

"That was sort of strange, wasn't it?" asked Henry. "It seemed as if she didn't know where she was going."

"She's a very unusual woman," said Jessie. "Now we'd better get to the store and figure out what we're going to make her for dinner."

***

A short while later, the Aldens were at the local grocery store, pushing their cart to the checkout counter. They had decided to make hamburgers, corn on the cob, and a green salad, and they had gotten ice cream for dessert. Just then, Jessie spotted Andrea Barton at the counter ahead of them. She was smiling and humming to herself.

"Hello again," Jessie said.

"Hello!" Andi said. Almost instantly her happy face grew serious. "Oh, um, I'm glad I ran into you," she said. Her voice sounded tense and nervous.

"So are we," Benny said. "Your concert the other day was great."

"Thanks," Andi said, a smile filling her face. But then she grew serious again. "I just wanted to ask you, um…"

"Yes?" Violet asked.

"Well, nothing really, just..." She twirled a piece of hair. "Please don't say anything to Ezra about what I said yesterday, okay?"

"Sure," said Jessie. After a moment she asked, "But what did you say?"

Andi laughed briefly. "Never mind," she said, picking up her bag of groceries. "I'll see you around."

The Aldens paid for their groceries and left the store. Their arms were loaded down with grocery bags.

"What do you think Andi meant when she asked us not to say anything to Ezra?" Violet asked as they walked.

"I was wondering that too," said Jessie. "Was it that she told us she came in a lot to practice?"

"I thought it was about losing her glasses," said Benny.

"And losing the new music she bought," Henry added. "Remember she said Ezra probably wouldn't have liked it?"

"I wonder why she always seems so nervous," Violet said. "She's so nice and so talented. She should be happier."

When they got back to their suite, Jessie began shaping the ground beef into round patties. Henry and Violet washed and tore the lettuce and cut up carrots and tomatoes for the salad. Benny husked the corn and put a large pot of water on the stove. They would wait until dinnertime, when Grandfather came home, to boil the corn and fry the burgers. After the food was prepared, the children set the table and placed some flowers in the center.

"That looks nice," Violet said.

As they waited for Grandfather to arrive, the children got out a deck of cards and began to play.

"I can't stop thinking about the buried treasure," Jessie said as she shuffled the cards.

"Me either!" said Benny, his eyes aglow.

"Do you think that someone we know is the person who's after it?" asked Henry.

"Like who?" said Violet.

"Oh, I don't know," Henry said. "But some of the people we've met here have acted, well, strangely. Like Ezra."

Jessie began to deal the cards. "You think he's the one who found the letter and started looking in the tower?"

"Could be," Henry said. "Maybe that's why he got so angry when we asked him if anyone goes up there at night—because *he's* going up there, and he doesn't want anyone to know."

"But he didn't seem to know about the treasure at all," said Violet. "In fact, he was surprised that we actually found something in the clock."

"Hmmm, that's true," Jessie said. "But he could have been pretending."

Henry agreed. "He helped us out—but maybe that was so he could find out for himself where the key was hidden."

"I've been wondering about Andi," said Violet, picking up her cards. "Ezra said everything was okay until she started working there. Maybe she took the job in the tower so she could look for the treasure."

"Go on," Jessie said thoughtfully.

Violet continued, "Remember that day she was searching for something and she said it was her glasses? Maybe it was really that letter that she'd misplaced, and then we found it not long afterward."

"And today in the grocery store she was certainly worried about something," said Jessie. "She seems to be keeping something secret from Ezra."

"And Ezra seems to be hiding something from us," said Benny. "Something about going up in the tower at night."

"But remember, whoever went up there broke the carillon," said Henry. "Why would Ezra do that?"

"That's true," said Benny.

"Don't forget the muddy footprint," Henry said. "Neither Ezra nor Andi seem to wear sneakers."

The children stopped talking and concentrated on their game of cards for a moment. After Jessie had taken her turn, she said, "Don Dixon has also been acting strangely. He got so upset about that old book, and we were being really careful with it. He still seemed upset about it today when we saw him on the Quad. Maybe he was afraid we'd read something about the treasure in there. And then on the tour he asked so many questions about the clock tower. I bet it's because he was trying to figure out where the treasure is hidden."

"But Don is Joel's son and Joel is Grandfather's good friend," Violet pointed out. "Do you really think he'd act so sneaky?"

Jessie shrugged. "I don't know. I really don't."

"Well, I do know one thing," Benny said, laying down his cards to show the others. "I won!"

***

A short while later, Grandfather returned from the concert. As he came in the door, he was humming lightly under his breath.

"How was the concert?" Violet asked.

"It was wonderful," Grandfather said. "It was a choral group, and they sang some lovely songs from when I was young. Reminded me of your grandmother." He smiled fondly at the memory. "At the end, they sang the school's fight song and anthem."

"That sounds great," Jessie commented.

"How did your treasure hunt go?" Grandfather asked.

"We didn't get very far," Violet said. "We went to ask Professor Meyer for help, but she was busy."

"So we invited her for dinner tonight," Henry said. "I hope that's all right with you."

"Sure it is," Grandfather said. "I was just noticing how nicely you set the table. I was wondering if that was just for me."

"We went into town and bought some burgers and corn," Jessie said.

"She should be here soon," Violet added. "Did you see her at the concert? She said she was going."

"She was at the concert?" Grandfather thought for a moment. "I must have missed her. I'm surprised, though, because it wasn't a very large room."

"Hmmmm," said Henry, pulling Violet aside. "I wonder if she really was going to the concert, or if she just made that up when we told her Grandfather would be there. She didn't seem to know much about it."

"But why would she make it up?" asked Violet.

"I don't know. It might have something to

do with her 'special project,'" said Henry.

Just then there was a knock at the door.

"That must be Professor Meyer now," Grandfather said, going to greet her.

"Hello," he said as he opened the door.

"Nice to see you, Jimmy," Professor Meyer said as she came into the suite. "Hello, children," she called. "How pretty the table looks!"

"Come sit down," Jessie said. "Dinner will be ready in a few minutes."

"Did you enjoy the concert?" Violet asked.

"The concert?" Professor Meyer looked puzzled.

Henry shot a look at the others as if to say, *See? She didn't even go to the concert.*

But after a moment the professor said, "Oh, the concert! It was lovely."

"It was, wasn't it?" Grandfather agreed.

With help from Grandfather, the children fried the burgers, boiled the corn, and tossed the salad. Soon everything was ready.

"This all looks so good!" Professor Meyer said, sitting down to eat.

The food was delicious, and the conversation

lively. Professor Meyer told them lots of good stories about the old days at Goldwin. It wasn't until they had finished eating that the children decided to bring up Joshua Chambers's letters.

As soon as the table was cleared, Henry said, "Professor Meyer, we wanted to ask you about a couple of old letters and a key we found."

"Oh, yes, you did have a question for me," she recalled.

Violet handed the letters to the professor. "Oh, how interesting," she said, carefully unfolding the yellowed papers. "Wherever did you find these?"

"Up in the clock tower," Benny said.

Professor Meyer had put the letters down on the table and was feeling around in her pockets for something. "Now, where did I..." she muttered to herself.

"Are you looking for something?" Henry asked.

"My glasses," she said.

"They're on top of your head," Benny said, trying to keep from laughing.

"They are?" she said. She put her hand up

and touched them. "Oh, goodness, you're right!" She laughed heartily, and the others joined her. "Silly me!"

"I think those are the same glasses as Mrs. McGregor's—our housekeeper," said Benny.

"They are?" Grandfather asked.

"Yeah, I think so," Benny said. "They look so familiar."

"Let's see these letters," Professor Meyer said. She read the first letter quickly, and then turned to the second, and studied it as well. "So that's what happened to it," she said softly to herself.

"What did you say?" Benny asked.

"Oh, um, nothing," Professor Meyer said quickly.

The Aldens explained how they had found the first letter, and the research they had done in the library. "That was some good thinking," Professor Meyer said to Jessie. "The library is a wonderful resource. Maybe you'll be a professor one day. We spend a lot of time in the library looking things up."

Jessie blushed with pride.

"Then we went back to the tower and

found the second note and the key," Benny explained. "Can you help us figure out where the treasure is buried?"

"I don't know," said Professor Meyer. "It's very mysterious, isn't it? I remember a long time ago…" She went off on a long story about the old days. When she'd finished, she looked at her watch. "Oh, my, look what time it is. Well, I've imposed on your hospitality long enough." She pushed her chair back from the table and stood up.

The family walked Professor Meyer to the door. "So you don't have any more ideas about how we can find this treasure?" Benny asked, disappointed.

"No, I really don't," she said.

"Okay," Benny said, looking sad.

Professor Meyer thought for a moment. "There is one thing," she said slowly. "Let me see the second letter again."

Violet handed it to her.

The professor studied the letter. "No, I can't be sure," she said to herself. "But it could be…"

"What?" Benny asked excitedly.

Professor Meyer pointed to the letter. "See here where he talks about North and South?"

The children nodded.

"Morrill Hall and McGraw Hall used to be called North Building and South Building because of where they're located on the Quad," she said. "Maybe that's what he means by North and South." Professor Meyer looked around at the children. "Who knows?"

A moment later, she was gone.

"That was a lovely dinner you children made," Grandfather said. "And I certainly enjoyed having the chance to talk to Professor Meyer some more."

"I wonder if she's right about North and South meaning Morrill and McGraw," said Benny.

"In the letter, Chambers says, 'Set yourself between North and South,'" Violet said. "It sounds as if he's telling his son to stand between those two buildings."

"That's where the treasure is?" Benny asked.

"I guess so," said Henry.

"Come on, let's go!" Benny cried.

"Wait a minute, wait a minute," Henry said. "The letter says to stand there when the clock strikes six in the morning."

"But why does it matter?" Benny asked.

"I don't know," said Henry. "But that's what the letter says."

"It looks like we're getting up early tomorrow!" said Jessie.

CHAPTER 8

The Tower Points the Way

"Jessie, Violet, wake up," said Benny.

Violet opened her eyes and sat up. "What time is it?"

"Five thirty," said Benny.

"Ugh," said Violet, falling back onto her pillow.

Benny had set his little alarm clock for five-thirty to give them time to get dressed and get to the Quad by six. He and Henry had already put on their clothes.

Jessie sprang out of bed. "Come on, Violet!

Let's go find the treasure!"

The children reached the Quad a few minutes before six. They walked past the building under construction, with its wooden frame and piles of dirt. When they had reached the lawn in between McGraw and Morrill Halls, they stopped and looked around.

"I feel as if we should be looking for something," Violet said, "but I'm not sure what."

"I know what you mean," Jessie agreed.

Then they heard the clock strike. *Ding, ding, ding,* it began. The children looked around. *Ding, ding,* it continued. *Ding.* The last chime hung in the air.

"Well?" Benny asked. "The clock has struck six. Now what?"

"I don't know," said Henry.

"Let's look at the letter again," suggested Violet.

"I'm hot," said Benny. It was an unusually hot day and he had run straight up the hill to the Quad because he was so excited. "Let's sit down in the shade while we read it." He walked over and sat down in the shadow of the tower, which cut across the Quad in a long line.

As they all sat down, Violet pulled out the letter. "It says, 'The tower will point the way.' What does that mean?"

Suddenly Jessie said, "That's it! Look at the tower's shadow!"

The shadow was a long thin rectangle, with a point at the top because of the pointed roof.

"Oh, my goodness!" Violet exclaimed. "It looks like a giant arrow."

"It really is pointing the way!" Benny said.

"It looks like it's pointing to a spot right here," Henry said, marking the ground with his foot.

"That must be where it's buried!" said Jessie.

"And that would explain why we had to be here at six on a summer morning—the tower's shadow would be different at different times of the year and different times of the day," Henry pointed out.

The children looked at one another, their faces glowing with excitement.

"What are we waiting for?" Benny cried.

"Let's start digging!"

"I don't think we can just start digging up the middle of the Quad," Violet said uncertainly.

"No, I don't think so, either," said Henry.

"But we can't just do nothing!" Benny said. "There's a treasure down there."

"There *might* be a treasure," Jessie reminded him. "Someone might already have found it."

"We need to ask someone if it's okay to dig," Henry said.

"Look at that truck." Violet pointed off to the side of the Quad, where some men in green jumpsuits were trimming bushes. "It says 'Goldwin University Grounds Crew' on the side. They might be good people to ask."

The children ran over to where the men were working. Jessie noticed that one of the men had a walkie-talkie and a clipboard. He seemed to be in charge. When she got closer she saw his jumpsuit had the words HEAD GROUNDSKEEPER embroidered over the left breast pocket.

"Excuse me," she said to the man. "We have a question to ask you."

"What can I do for you, young lady?" he asked.

"I know this is going to sound strange, but we'd like to dig a hole in the Quad, over there where the tower's shadow ends." Jessie turned and pointed. "Would that be okay?"

"What are you doing, searching for buried treasure?" the man asked, chuckling. "Normally I'd say no, but they're going to be digging up this area anyway this week, to put in a water line for the new construction. So it's fine with me!"

"Thank you!" Jessie said.

"You can even borrow our shovels, if you like," he said, motioning to some shovels in the back of the truck.

Jessie looked around at the others.

"That would be great," Henry said as he and Jessie each took two large shovels out of the truck. "We'll bring them back in a little while."

The four children walked back to the spot between Morrill and McGraw, carrying the shovels. When they got to the spot where the shadow seemed to be pointing, they started digging. Henry pushed his shovel in first, pulling up a big pile of dirt. The others joined in.

All of a sudden Benny stopped shoveling.

"What's the matter, Benny?" Jessie asked as she lifted a shovelful of dirt and dumped it in the growing pile.

"I was just thinking about Professor Meyer's glasses," Benny said, going back to his digging.

"Why were you thinking about that?" Henry asked.

"Remember last night I said her glasses were the same as Mrs. McGregor's?" Benny said.

The other children nodded.

"I just realized something. That's not why they looked familiar. It's because they're the same glasses we found up in the clock tower," he said.

"Really?" Jessie asked. "That would mean Professor Meyer has been up in the tower at night. Maybe *she* dropped the letter!"

"Remember when we showed her the letter?" Violet asked. "She said, 'So that's what happened to it.'"

"And she wears sneakers," Benny said excited-ly. "That would explain that muddy footprint."

"Maybe this is the 'special project' she'd said she was working on," Henry said. "Remember—she said she was always hoping to make a little more money. Finding a treasure would certainly do that!"

"But she seems so nice," Jessie said. "I can't believe she would be up to no good."

"And how could she find a treasure if she can't even find her own glasses?" Benny asked.

"Maybe that's just an act," said Henry. "Maybe she just pretends to be nice and sweet and forgetful, when she really knows exactly what she's doing."

By now they had dug a hole about a foot deep. But there was no sign of a treasure.

"What if this isn't the right spot?" Benny asked, taking a break and leaning on his shovel. It was hard work, and the children were all getting tired and sweaty.

"Or what if the treasure is already gone?" asked Violet.

"Let's dig a little while longer before we give up," Henry suggested.

"Okay," the others agreed.

A moment later, Jessie's shovel hit something hard. "I think there's something down here," she said excitedly. The others began digging in that spot as quickly as they could.

"Yes, there's definitely something hard here!" Violet said.

But when they'd pushed the dirt away, all they found was a large rock.

"Oh, no!" Benny said. "All that work for nothing. I bet it's not here."

Refusing to stop, Henry pushed his shovel into the ground one more time. The children all heard a loud clanging sound.

"What was that?" asked Benny.

"I don't know, but it didn't sound like dirt, and it didn't sound like a rock," said Henry.

Jessie, Violet, and Benny all came over and helped dig. At last they could see what Henry's shovel had hit. It was the top of a large metal box!

"The treasure!" Benny cried.

"I don't believe it," said Jessie. "It's really here!"

Getting down on their hands and knees, the children used their hands to clear the dirt away from the top and sides of the metal box. Then they dug more around the sides, until at last they had found the bottom corners of the box. After a little more digging, Henry and Jessie were able to reach down and put their arms around the big box, and put their hands underneath. "It's heavy," Henry said as he and Jessie slowly lifted.

"Yeah," Jessie gasped. Slowly the two lifted the large metal box out of the hole.

"Wow, look at that," said Violet.

The front of the box had a large heavy lock on it. "It's a good thing we have the key," said Benny.

"Let's hope it fits," Violet said, pulling it from her pocket.

She slipped the key into the old lock and turned. The lock clicked open.

The children looked at one another with anticipation. What would they find inside?

"Here goes," Henry said. He and Jessie stood on either side of the box and slowly lifted the heavy lid.

Inside the box they found several bundles wrapped in cloth. Henry bent down and began unwrapping one. Inside was an antique silver teapot. He unwrapped another bundle and found a collection of silverware. A large cloth bag was filled with heavy gold and silver coins and jewelry.

The children just stood and stared, too stunned to speak. They had known they were on a treasure hunt, but they had never imagined they'd really find a treasure.

"I don't believe it!" said Jessie.

"A real treasure," said Benny.

"But it's not ours," Violet pointed out.

"No, we'll have to return it to Joshua Chambers's family," said Henry.

"But still, I can't believe we found a real treasure," said Benny.

"You sure did," said a voice behind them. "And you beat me to it!"

The children turned to see Julia Meyer standing behind them.

"Professor Meyer!" said Henry.

CHAPTER 9

The Professor's Secret Project

The children looked at Professor Meyer and then looked at one another. Was she after the treasure?

"I thought about that second letter all night," Professor Meyer said. "When I woke up this morning, I realized that the shadow of the tower would point to the treasure! I came here as quickly as I could."

"Are you here for the treasure?" Benny asked boldly. "Is this what you meant by your 'special project'?"

"Indeed it is," the professor said with a mysterious smile. "But not the way you think. We need to talk. Please come up to the top of the clock tower with me. Bring the box."

The children weren't sure what to do. For a moment, they just stood there. Was Professor Meyer trying to steal the treasure?

At last Henry spoke up. "Come on. Let's go see what Professor Meyer has to tell us."

First Violet ran over to return the shovels to the grounds crew. Then Henry and Jessie each picked up a side of the treasure box and carried it along with them. When they reached the bottom of the tower, they put the box down to rest their arms.

The children climbed the winding stairs very slowly, because of the treasure box. They stopped a couple of times so that Henry and Jessie could put the box down and rest.

At last they reached the top of the tower. As Professor Meyer pushed the door open, they were surprised to see their grandfather, Joel, and Don all waiting inside. Ezra was there too, having just finished the morning concert.

"Hello, children!" Grandfather said. "What

have you got there?" The adults all crowded around the heavy metal box, which still had clumps of dirt clinging to it.

"Grandfather! Wait until you see!" Benny cried.

"What are you doing here?" Jessie asked.

"I got a phone call from Professor Meyer this morning asking me to meet her here," he explained. "Joel and Don were over having coffee, so they came along."

Grandfather looked at the box. "Is this the treasure you were hunting for?"

"It is!" cried Benny. "It really is!"

"What? You found the treasure? Where?" Don exclaimed. He was walking slowly around the large box, looking at it curiously.

"In the Quad," Jessie said. "The grounds-keeper lent us shovels and we dug it up!"

"Let's open it!" Don said.

Slowly Henry lifted the lid of the box, revealing the cloth-wrapped bundles. One by one, he unwrapped the bundles for everyone to see. Don bent over and picked each piece up, turning it over in his hands, but saying nothing.

"Look at that beautiful pocket watch!" Ezra said.

"That silver goblet is stunning," said the professor.

"But how did you know the children were going to find this treasure?" Grandfather asked.

"Remember they showed me the letters last night?" Professor Meyer began. "I didn't figure out everything that second letter meant until this morning. I looked out at the sunrise and suddenly everything fell into place! I realized that the tower's shadow would point the way! When I called, I was planning to tell them, but they'd already figured it out. They're your grandchildren, Jimmy, so I should have known they'd be smart. I asked you to join me here so that I could tell you about my project."

"Yes, please, tell us," Jessie said.

"I have been treasure hunting myself," she began.

"We thought so!" Benny cried.

Jessie explained. "We found this letter up here in the tower, and we saw lights in the middle of the night. So we figured out that someone was up here looking for the treasure. And when we found your glasses…"

"But I was not searching for the sort of treasure you see before you," Professor Meyer went on. "I have been searching for information about the past."

"Why are you looking for that?" Benny asked.

"I am writing a book," the professor said. "A history of Goldwin University."

"Is that how you're going to make money?" asked Jessie.

"Yes, a little bit, if I can sell a few copies," Professor Meyer said. "I have done a great deal of research. Some of my research has been up here, looking at these old photos."

"So that's when you left your glasses up here!" Henry said.

"Indeed I did," Professor Meyer said. "But I haven't been up here late at night. I've only come during the day. Much of my research has been speaking with people connected with Goldwin. One such person is Laurence Chambers, the great-great-grandnephew of the

university's first president, Joshua Chambers."
The professor paused and looked around.
"He told me an interesting tale. He said that
all of the family's valuables were mysteriously
missing after the Civil War. There was a story
in the family that his great-great-granduncle,
Joshua Chambers, had hidden them to keep
them safe from the army. But no one ever
knew for sure what had happened to them. So
when I read that letter last night, it answered a
lot of questions—but raised many more."

"Is that why you said, 'So that's what
happened to it,' when we showed you the
letters?" Violet said.

"Yes," the professor said. "I had been
wondering where the family wealth had
gone."

"But if you weren't the one who had the
letter in the first place," Henry said, "then
who did?"

"And who was up here in the middle of the
night?" asked Jessie.

Just then the door burst open and Andi
came rushing in. She seemed surprised by
the crowd of people in the tower. She looked

even more surprised when she saw the silver and gold objects laid out on the desk.

"Look at the treasure we found!" Benny said.

"You found this?" Andi asked. "Where? How?"

"We found two letters with clues in them—" Benny began, but before he could explain, Andi burst out crying. She dropped her bag and sank down in a chair, her face in her hands.

"Miss Barton!" Ezra said. "What is the matter?"

Andi took a deep breath and tried to collect herself. She looked around at all the faces staring at her.

"I'm sorry, it's nothing..." she began.

Jessie whispered to Henry, "Do you think she's upset because she was the one looking for the treasure?"

Henry shrugged his shoulders.

"Oh, Ezra," Andi was saying. "I'm upset because I came here to quit. I can't be your assistant anymore."

"But whyever not?" Ezra asked.

"Because I'm no good," Andi said. "I keep losing things, like the new music I bought. And I don't play well enough. I've been sneaking in here for extra practice, but I didn't want you to know."

"Don't play well enough?" Ezra said. "You're great! In fact, you're so good, I'm afraid they're going to give you my job when you graduate! I'm getting old, and you're bringing in that exciting newfangled music."

"I thought you didn't like the new music," Andi said.

Ezra looked at her sheepishly. "I admit it took me a little while to get used to the idea. But now I really enjoy it." He paused. "In fact, the reason you couldn't find your music is because I borrowed it." He looked at the Aldens. "I may be the one you've seen up here at night. I came up here once to try out Miss Barton's new music, but I didn't want anyone to know."

Andi beamed. "I'm so relieved. I thought you were disappointed with me."

"Well, you could try to be a little more organized," Ezra said. "But you're an excellent carillon player."

"I'll try harder," Andi said. "And I'll help you with the new music. I'm just so honored to be working with a gifted carillon player like you."

"Now we know who was up in the tower those nights," Henry said.

"Actually, I only came up here one night," Ezra said.

The children looked at one another, confused. "But we saw a light up here on two different nights."

At that moment Don came forward and cleared his throat. "I think I have some explaining to do," he said. "I was the one you saw up here in the tower the other night."

Chapter 10

A Reward for the Children

"*You* were the one?" Joel asked in disbelief.

"Yes, I was the one who found the letter—and then left it up here," Don said.

"Where did you find it?" Benny wanted to know.

"It was tucked inside that antique book my father gave me," Don said.

"So that's why you didn't want us looking at the book," Jessie said.

"That's right—I kept the letter in the book," he said. "Until I brought it up here. I didn't want you looking in the book because I was afraid you might see it."

"That day we saw you on the Quad and you started to ask us about the book—" Jessie recalled.

"By then I'd realized I'd lost the letter," Don said. "I was going to ask if you had seen it. But then I decided I'd better not mention it, or I'd have a lot of explaining to do."

Then Joel spoke up. "So that's why you were so eager to come up here to visit. You wanted to find the treasure."

"Yes," Don said. "I went up into the tower in the middle of the night to search. I only had a flashlight on, so I didn't think anyone would see me."

Suddenly Violet remembered something. "It was your muddy footprint we saw, wasn't it?" she said, looking down at the sneakers Don was wearing.

"I suppose it must have been," Don agreed. "When I was searching around up here, I tried to look inside and behind the carillon—I'm afraid I may have broken some of the wires by accident when I leaned on them. I even went up to look at the bells and unscrewed some of the parts to see if somehow a treasure could be hidden inside."

"That was a terrible thing you did," Ezra said angrily. "It took me a long time to fix the carillon."

Don's face turned red, and he looked at the floor. "I'm so sorry," he said quietly. "I wasn't thinking. I'd come so far, and I didn't want to leave empty-handed. I'll repay you for the time you spent repairing them."

"What I don't understand is: Why were you being so secretive? Why not tell the university what you'd found?" Professor Meyer asked.

"I know what I did wasn't right. But I never intended to keep the money. I just wanted to find the treasure." Don looked at his father.

"Still playing detective?" Joel asked.

"I guess so," Don said sadly. "I'm sorry."

"Well, I'm glad all the mysteries have been solved," the professor said. "Thanks to the Aldens." She smiled at the children, who smiled back proudly.

"What's going to happen to the treasure?"

Benny asked.

"We'll have to notify the Chambers family," Professor Meyer said. "For now, perhaps we should bring the treasure to the president's office for safekeeping."

"That sounds like a good idea," said Jessie.

***

The next day, the Aldens were getting ready to leave Goldwin and return home. Their suitcases were packed and ready. The family was just finishing up lunch in the dining hall.

"I've enjoyed being here again after all these years, but it will be good to get back to Greenfield," Grandfather said.

"I agree," said Jessie.

"I miss Mrs. McGregor's cooking," Benny said.

"Look, there's Professor Meyer," Violet called out as they stood up to leave.

Grandfather waved to her and she came right over. "I'm glad I found you before you left," she said. "I spoke with Laurence Chambers last night. He was overjoyed to hear that you had found the family valuables—he couldn't believe it. In fact, he took the first flight here and arrived this morning."

"Really?" Henry said. "Has he seen the treasure yet?"

"Yes, and it was more wonderful than he'd imagined," the professor said. "He'd like to meet you and thank you in person."

The children looked at one another, their eyes glowing.

"We'd love to," said Jessie.

The Aldens went with the professor up to the top of the tower one last time. When they reached the top, a tall dark-haired man was standing looking out the window. As he turned to face them, Violet said, "You look like your great-great-granduncle."

"Do I?" Mr. Chambers asked.

"Yes," Henry agreed. "We saw a picture of him in a book."

"And you must be the Aldens," Mr. Chambers said. "I can't thank you enough for finding my family heirlooms."

"It was our pleasure," Jessie assured him.

"I'd like to give each of you a small piece of the treasure," Mr. Chambers went on. He held out his hand and showed the children four old gold coins. "Will you accept these as your reward?"

The children were too stunned to speak. As he handed each of them a coin, Grandfather said, "They're speechless. I think that means they accept your offer."

At last the children remembered their manners. "Thank you!" they each said.

"As I was saying, it is the sentimental value, not the money, that matters to me," Mr. Chambers said. "Last night I discussed with my family what to do with this treasure.

"As you know, my family has always been very devoted to this university. We will keep a few pieces, but the rest we are going to donate to Goldwin. We'll be putting some of the antiques, like the goblets, on display."

"What about the gold and silver?" asked Henry.

"My cousins and I discussed what to do with it," Mr. Chambers said. "My great-great-granduncle was quite fond of music, especially the carillon. You may have figured that out from his letters."

"Yes, it sounded that way," said Jessie.

"My family would like to use this money to add some new bells," said Mr. Chambers.

"What a wonderful idea," Ezra said. "Thank you so very much."

"Our music will sound even more beautiful," Andi said excitedly.

"Your great-great-granduncle would have been proud," Ezra said.

"Thank you for calling me," Mr. Chambers said to Professor Meyer. Then he turned to the Aldens. "And thank you again, for finding my family's treasure."

"You're welcome," said Henry.

"Anytime you need a treasure found, just call us!" said Benny with a smile. "We're always ready for a treasure hunt."

THE BOXCAR CHILDREN

THE GHOST IN THE FIRST ROW

Created by
GERTRUDE CHANDLER WARNER

Contents

CHAPTER 1

Lady Chadwick's Riddle

"Is it really haunted, Grandfather?" asked six-year-old Benny, his eyes huge.

"Haunted?" James Alden looked puzzled, but only for a moment. "Oh, I suppose you children heard me on the phone?"

Jessie poured more milk into Benny's glass. "Yes, you were talking to Aunt Jane about the Trap-Door Theater, Grandfather," she explained. At twelve, Jessie often acted like a mother to her younger brother and sister.

Violet, who was ten, looked up. "Benny

heard you say it was haunted, Grandfather."

Fourteen-year-old Henry shook his head. "Ghosts don't exist, Benny," he said. He sounded very sure.

The four Alden children—Henry, Jessie, Violet, and Benny—were sitting around the dining room table with their grandfather. They were discussing their upcoming visit to nearby Elmford. Aunt Jane had invited the children to stay with her while Uncle Andy was away on business.

Grandfather put down his fork. "The Trap-Door Theater was closed years ago, Benny," he explained. "Sometimes people start talking about ghosts when a building's been empty for a long time."

"That's true," said Mrs. McGregor, as she came into the room. "It's been called the haunted theater for as long as I can remember." She placed a bowl of salad on the table. "From what I've heard, they've done a wonderful job fixing up the old place."

Grandfather nodded. "That building was quite an eyesore," he said. "Now it looks just like it did when it was first built in the late 1800s."

"Aunt Jane bought tickets for opening night," Violet told their housekeeper, her eyes shining. "We'll be seeing a mystery play."

"And mysteries are our specialty!" added Benny, sounding just as excited as his sister. There was nothing the children loved better than a mystery, and together they'd managed to solve quite a few.

"I bet you'll have that mystery figured out before the last act, Benny," guessed Mrs. McGregor.

"Well, I am very good at sniffing out clues," Benny admitted.

Henry couldn't help laughing. "Benny, you're almost as good at sniffing out clues as you are at sniffing out food!"

"Right!" Benny gave his brother the thumbs-up sign. The youngest Alden was known for his appetite. He was always hungry.

"Aunt Jane had a hunch you'd enjoy a good whodunit," said Grandfather, as Mrs. McGregor walked out of the room.

"A what?" Benny looked puzzled.

"A whodunit," Henry repeated. "That's another name for a mystery, Benny."

"Oh, I get it," said Benny, catching on. "They call it a whodunit because you figure out who did it. Right?"

"Right," said Grandfather, as he passed the salad along. "And the play's supposed to be a first-rate whodunit. At least, that's what Aunt Jane tells me."

"One thing's for sure," said Jessie. "It'll be great to see Aunt Jane again."

"I'll second that!" Henry said.

"Yes, it's been a while since you've had a visit." Grandfather helped himself to the mashed potatoes.

Just then, Watch ran over, wagging his tail.

"Sorry, Watch," Violet said, petting their family dog softly on the head. "You can't go with us this time."

"Dogs aren't allowed on the train," said Benny.

"Besides," put in Violet, "you need to keep Grandfather and Mrs. McGregor company while we're gone."

"And look after our boxcar," added Henry.

After their parents died, the four Alden children had run away. For a while, their home was an old boxcar in the woods. But then their grandfather, James Alden, had found them. He brought his grandchildren to live with him in his big white house in Greenfield. Even the boxcar was given a special place in the backyard. The children often used it as a clubhouse.

"I'll drop you off at the train station after lunch tomorrow," said Grandfather. "Aunt Jane will be waiting for you when you arrive in Elmford."

"Thanks, Grandfather," said Jessie. "We'll pack tonight, then we won't be rushed in the morning."

The other Aldens smiled at each other. They could always count on Jessie to be organized.

Violet was wondering about something.

"Grandfather, why was the Trap-Door Theater left empty for such a long time?"

"Well, when the theater was first built, Violet," said Grandfather, "it was Elmford's pride and joy. Tickets were always sold out. But as the years went by, the building needed repairs. It slowly became more and more rundown. Soon people didn't want to go there anymore."

"Why didn't they do the repairs?" Benny wondered.

"The town of Elmford didn't have the money, Benny. The council finally closed the theater down."

"How did they finally get the money to fix it up?" Jessie wondered.

"When Alice Duncan died, she left her money to the town to restore the place," said Grandfather. "Alice was one of Aunt Jane's neighbors."

"What a wonderful thing to do!" said Violet. Jessie nodded. "She saved the old theater."

"For now, anyway." Grandfather put down his fork. "Everyone's hoping the theater will bring tourists into town. But…"

"If it doesn't," guessed Henry, "they'll close it down again?"

"I'm afraid so, Henry. But if the theater brings tourists into town, it'll be good for everyone."

"That makes sense," Henry said after

a moment's thought. "There'll be more shoppers going in and out of the stores. Right, Grandfather?"

"Right." Grandfather nodded.

"Oh, I'm sure the play will be a success," said Violet.

Benny was quick to agree. "Everybody likes a mystery!"

***

True to her word, Aunt Jane was waiting for the Aldens when their train pulled into Elmford the next day.

"I brought my binoculars for the play, Aunt Jane!" Benny shouted, running up and giving her a hug. Laughing, Aunt Jane returned the hug.

"Don't worry, Benny," she said. "We'll be sitting in the first row. I don't think you'll need binoculars."

"We can't wait to see what the theater looks like now," Violet said.

Henry loaded the suitcases into the car and they all got inside.

"Actually, you can take a peek at it right away," Aunt Jane said. "The theater is just

around the corner, so you can see it from the outside. It's been completely done over."

"Thanks to your neighbor," said Henry, sitting up front beside Aunt Jane. "Alice Duncan, I mean."

"Yes, Alice was a great fan of the theater," said Aunt Jane. "And a wonderful friend."

Violet didn't like to hear the note of sadness in Aunt Jane's voice. She was trying to think of something cheery to say, but Jessie spoke first.

"I bet Alice would be pleased with all the work that's been done," she said.

"Yes, I think she would." Aunt Jane smiled at Jessie through the rearview mirror. "In the old days, Alice had a seat in the first row for every mystery play. And she always brought her knitting and a bag of popcorn with her for intermission."

"Wow," said Benny. "I guess Alice liked mysteries."

"She sure did, Henry." Aunt Jane nodded. "As a matter of fact, she even wrote her own mystery plays."

The children were surprised to hear this.

"Alice Duncan was a writer?" Jessie asked.

"She sure was," said Aunt Jane. "Whenever we had a cup of tea together, she'd tell me about her latest codes and clues."

That sounded like fun to Benny. "I bet she was a good writer."

"The best, Benny," said Aunt Jane. "And she always put a surprise twist in the last act."

"Were any of her plays performed in the Trap-Door Theater?" Jessie wondered.

"It was always Alice's dream to have one of her plays performed." Aunt Jane sighed. "But sadly, her dream never came true."

"What a shame!" said Violet.

"Alice wanted to give other writers the chance she never had," Aunt Jane went on. "That's why she left her money to the town— on one condition."

At this, the children were curious. "What was the condition?" Henry wondered.

"That a contest be held every summer. The winner would get a cash award," said Aunt Jane, "and the winning play would be performed at the Trap-Door Theater."

"Cool!" said Benny.

"The winner this year is a local college student, Tricia Jenkins. And from what I hear, she can really use the money."

"Oh?" Henry asked.

"Yes, apparently Tricia's putting herself through school," Aunt Jane told them. "She earns extra money working at her computer. They say she's an expert typist."

"So, it's Tricia's play we'll be seeing on opening night?" Jessie wondered.

"Yes." Aunt Jane nodded. "And I'm really looking forward to it. The judges were all very impressed that someone so young could write such a fine play."

"Then it's bound to be a big hit," Henry concluded.

"We're keeping our fingers crossed, Henry. Nobody wants the theater to close down again," said Aunt Jane.

"Well, guess what, Aunt Jane?" Benny piped up. "I'm going to clap extra hard at the end of the play—just in case."

"In case what, Benny?" asked Henry, looking over his shoulder.

"In case the theater really is haunted," said

Benny. "The clapping will drown out all the booing from the ghosts."

"That's a good one, Benny," Henry said, as everyone burst out laughing.

Chapter 2

The Haunted Theater

The Aldens drew in their breath as they pulled up in front of the Trap-Door Theater.

"Oh, it looks wonderful!" said Violet, as they climbed out of the car. She gazed admiringly at the stone building with its marble columns.

Henry let out a low whistle. "Awesome."

Aunt Jane looked pleased. "See those stone lions on either side of the ticket window? We thought they were lost forever," she said. "But then, one of the workmen came across them in a dark corner of the basement."

"That was lucky," said Benny.

"Yes, they were quite a find," Aunt Jane said, with a big smile. "Now the theater looks just like it did when it was first built."

"They really did a great job," said Jessie.

Aunt Jane agreed. "It's like stepping back in time," she said. "In fact, the mayor's planning to arrive by horse and buggy on opening night."

Henry's eyebrows shot up. "Wow, he's really getting into the spirit of things."

"Oh, yes," said Aunt Jane. "This is the biggest thing that's happened to Elmford in a long time."

Benny tilted his head back to look up at the sign above the doorway. "What does that say?" he wanted to know. The youngest Alden was just learning to read.

Jessie read the words on the billboard aloud. *"Lady Chadwick's Riddle*—Starring Fern Robson."

"You're not throwing your money away on tickets, are you?" Everyone whirled around as a middle-aged man with a mustache walked

toward them. He was wearing a business suit, and his dark hair was slicked back.

"Hello, Gil," Aunt Jane greeted him. "We were just checking out the theater." She introduced the children to Gil Diggs, the owner of the local movie theater.

"If you ask me, Alice wasted her money on this place."

Aunt Jane stared at Gil in surprise. "I think the Trap-Door Theater does the town proud."

"It's just a matter of time before they close it down again," Gil said, shaking his head. As he walked away, he called back over his shoulder, "Mark my words!"

"He doesn't seem very happy about the theater," said Benny.

"Gil has a lot on his mind these days," Aunt Jane explained. "It makes him seem a bit grumpy sometimes. You see, his movie theater hasn't been doing well lately."

Violet asked, "Why's that, Aunt Jane?"

"They opened a huge movie complex on the highway, Violet. Some of Gil's customers go there now. And on top of that, a lot of people would rather rent movies and watch them at home these days."

"That's true," said Henry. "We do that too."

Aunt Jane nodded. "I imagine Gil thinks the Trap-Door Theater will take away even more business. He doesn't seem to understand," she said, "that a successful theater will bring tourists into town."

"And that would be good for everyone's business," finished Henry, remembering what Grandfather had said.

"Exactly," said Aunt Jane. "But it'll take time for Gil to realize that, I'm afraid. Speaking of time," she added, "I'd better take Uncle Andy's watch to the jewelry store for repairs. I'll be right back."

While the children were waiting, they noticed a young woman in a hooded white top and track pants step out of the theater. She was wearing sunglasses, and her coppery red hair was pulled back into a ponytail. A tall man appeared seconds later, the sleeves of his white shirt rolled up above his elbows, and a pencil stuck behind his ear.

From where they were standing, the Aldens couldn't help overhearing their conversation.

"Hold on a minute," the young man was saying. "You're getting upset over nothing, Fern."

"How can you call it nothing? I have a good mind to walk out on—"

The man broke in, "I'm sure it's just somebody's idea of a joke."

"Well, if it's a joke," the woman shot back, "it's not a very funny one!"

"Her name is Fern," Henry whispered to the others. "She must be the actress starring in the play."

Jessie felt uncomfortable listening to the conversation. "Maybe we should walk over to the jewelry store," she suggested in a low voice. "It isn't nice to eavesdrop."

"Oh, here comes Aunt Jane now," said Violet.

"Jane Bean!" The young man waved a hand in the air as Aunt Jane approached. "You're just the person I wanted to see."

Aunt Jane introduced the children to Ray Shaw. He was the director of the Trap-Door

Theater. Then she said, "What can I do for you, Ray?"

"I was hoping I could stop by tonight," said Ray, "to pick up a few things from your shed."

"Of course!" Aunt Jane nodded. Then she turned to the children. "Alice left most of her belongings to the theater," she explained. "We're keeping them in the old shed out back."

"The workmen should be finished in the basement soon," said Ray. "Then we'll have a dry place to keep all the stage props."

"That's good," Aunt Jane told him. "As you know, the lock's been broken on that shed for years."

Ray laughed. "I don't think anybody would be interested in stealing old furniture," he told her.

"By the way," Aunt Jane added, "how are rehearsals going?"

"Don't ask!" The woman with the coppery red hair came over and joined their group. "I'm at the end of my rope."

Ray introduced everyone to Fern Robson who was playing the lead in *Lady Chadwick's Riddle.*

"This theater makes my hair stand on end," Fern went on, shivering a little. "I'm a bundle of nerves!"

Henry and Jessie exchanged glances. Why was Fern so upset?

"I have an idea," said Aunt Jane. "Why don't you both join us for dinner this evening? How does a barbecue sound?"

"Sounds great!" said Ray. "Count me in."

"Me too," said Fern. "I could use a break from the ghost world." The actress shivered a little.

The Aldens looked at one another. *The ghost world?* What on earth was Fern Robson talking about?

CHAPTER 3

Goose Bumps

"Fern is such a pretty name," Aunt Jane was saying, as they sat around the picnic table in the backyard.

"Oh, do you like it?" Fern's face broke into a smile. "You know, I couldn't make up my mind between Fern and Cassandra. But I decided to go with Fern."

Benny wrinkled up his forehead. "You named yourself?"

"Well, I'm really Susan. But I wanted a name with more pizzazz. Something that would look good up in lights."

"I think you made a great choice," Violet said.

"Thank you, Violet," said Fern. "Lots of people in show business change their names, you know. Even the winner of the playwriting contest changed her name. Isn't that true, Ray?"

Ray wiped some mustard from the corner of his mouth. "Well, she changed her nickname, at least."

"I was hoping to see my name first on the billboard," Fern went on. "Above the title of the play, I mean." She shot the director a look. "But I suppose that was hoping for too much."

Ray rolled his eyes, but he didn't say anything. Instead, he dished up another helping of potato salad.

Jessie couldn't help noticing that the Fern had hardly eaten a bite. She was only poking at her food with a fork.

The actress caught Jessie's look. "I'm afraid I have a nervous stomach," she said. "I can't stop thinking about all the strange things that have been happening at the theater."

Aunt Jane looked up in surprise. "What's been happening?"

Fern leaned forward and whispered, "The ghosts have been acting up."

"This isn't the time or the place—" Ray began.

Fern waved that away. "They've been using it for years, you know. It gives me goose bumps just to think about it!"

"What do you mean?" Benny's big eyes were round.

"I'm talking about the ghosts," Fern replied. "They've been using the theater to perform their plays."

The Aldens looked at one another. They were too stunned to speak.

"The ghosts aren't happy about the theater opening up again," Fern went on. "They don't want to share it with the public."

"You don't really believe that," said Henry. "Do you, Fern?"

"Take a look at the facts," Fern said.

Jessie stared at the actress. "What facts?"

"Well, for starters, things keep disappearing." Fern looked slowly around the table. "Then they show up in the oddest places."

"That's weird," said Benny. He was so interested in the conversation that he still hadn't taken a bite of his hamburger.

"Remember Lady Chadwick's hat?" Fern turned to look at Ray. "The one with the yellow marigolds on it?"

"I remember," said Ray. "We found it hanging from the chandelier in the lobby."

"What's a chandelier?" Benny wanted to know.

"It's a fancy ceiling light," Henry explained.

Violet giggled. She couldn't help it—it seemed so funny. "Well, if it's a ghost," she said, "it's a ghost with a sense of humor."

Everyone laughed—except Fern. "This isn't a laughing matter," she said with a frown. "The ghosts aren't happy."

"Now, Fern—" Ray started to say.

"It's no use shaking your head, Ray. You know it's true. And now Alice Duncan has joined the ghostly audience."

"*What?*" Aunt Jane almost choked on her lemonade.

"What makes you say that?" Jessie asked.

Fern leaned forward again. "One morning, we found a ball of yarn and some knitting needles on a seat in the first row."

Ray added, "We even found some popcorn on the floor."

"And as everybody knows," Fern said, "Alice always brought her knitting and a bag of popcorn to the theater with her. It was mentioned in all the newspaper articles after she died."

"But Alice wanted the theater opened up to the public again," Jessie pointed out. "Didn't she?"

Violet nodded. "That's why she left her money to the town."

"I guess she changed her mind." Fern suddenly pushed her plate away. "My stomach is too upset to eat. I'd better go home and lie down."

"Why don't you take the morning off tomorrow, Fern," Ray suggested. "We'll postpone the rehearsal until after lunch."

"I just might take you up on that," Fern said. "I need my beauty sleep." With that, she said good-bye and left.

Ray apologized for Fern's behavior. "She can be a handful sometimes. But she really is a wonderful actress."

"I can understand why Fern would be upset with so many strange things happening at the theater," said Aunt Jane. "I wonder who's responsible for all those pranks."

Jessie asked, "Did you notice anyone hanging around, Ray?"

"Only the actors and the stagehands." The director shook his head. "Nobody else."

"Are you sure?" Henry looked uncertain.

"Quite sure, Henry," said Ray. "We don't want anyone to see the theater until opening night."

Jessie had a thought. "What if somebody got in after everybody went home?"

Ray shook his head again. "I'm the only one with a key, Jessie."

"Maybe they didn't use a key," Benny suggested.

"I checked it out, Benny," Ray said. "It doesn't look like anyone broke in."

"Fern's right about one thing," said Violet.

"If it's a joke, it's not a very funny one."

"No, it's not," Ray agreed. "It's making everyone in the cast and crew very nervous. Nobody wants to stay late anymore. They're all afraid of ghosts."

"You've sure got your work cut out for you, Ray," said Aunt Jane.

"You can say that again." Ray nodded. "I hired some high school kids to help with the posters, but they were a no-show. I have a hunch they were scared away by the rumors of ghosts."

"Maybe we could lend a hand," volunteered Henry.

"Of course," agreed Jessie, while Violet and Benny nodded.

"Really?" Ray looked surprised—and pleased.

"We'd like to help," Violet said shyly.

Ray looked at the Aldens' eager faces. "Putting up posters around town is hard work," he warned them.

Aunt Jane laughed. "Oh, you don't know these children, Ray. There's nothing they like better than hard work."

"Well, I'd be very grateful for your help," Ray told them. "We need all the advertising we can get. I've been trying to get someone from the local paper to do a write-up. But... they're not interested unless it'll grab the readers' attention."

"Well, we'll help for sure," promised Benny. "When do we start?"

Ray was all smiles. "How does first thing in the morning sound?"

The Aldens thought it sounded just fine. After dinner, they walked over to the shed with Ray. Stepping inside, they found it overflowing with tables, chairs, trunks, and wooden boxes.

"Alice sure had lots of stuff," Benny said, looking around.

"She sure did," said Ray. "And we plan to make good use of it on stage."

Violet was taking a close look at an old typewriter. "Grandfather has one just like this in the attic."

"The keys stick and it won't print *w* at all," Ray told her. "But Alice used that old typewriter for years and years."

"She never used a computer?" Henry asked.

"Never. Not even when her fingers got weaker as she got older," said Ray. "She couldn't peck away at the typewriter keys anymore, but she still refused to use a computer. Instead, she recorded her plays on tape and hired a college student to type them up for her." Ray lifted the lid of a wooden box. "See? Alice's tapes are right here."

"The box is almost full," Benny noted.

Just then, Ray spotted a book on the windowsill. Reaching for it, he began to flip through the pages. "Looks like Alice's appointment book," he said. "Your aunt Jane's mentioned in here quite a bit."

"They were good friends," Jessie said.

"Alice's last entry seems to be about shoes." Ray read the words aloud: *Shoe won't fit. Tell PJ to make change.*

"I guess Alice bought a pair of shoes that were too small," Henry figured.

"I think your aunt Jane might like this book," said Ray. "It would be a nice keepsake."

"We'll make sure she gets it," Jessie promised.

Ray glanced around. "Now, there's something I can use!" He reached a bag down from a shelf. The label read: Plaster of Paris.

"What will you use it for?" Benny wanted to know.

"A prop for the play," Ray said, as he poured half of the white powder into an empty container. "We need a plaster cast of a footprint." Then he added, "That's how Lady Chadwick proves the butler did it."

"You make the cast with powder?" asked Benny.

Ray nodded. "You mix plaster of paris with water to form a paste," he said. "The paste hardens as it dries."

After helping Ray load up his pickup truck, the Aldens said good-bye, then headed back to the house.

"I wish we could figure out what's going on with the ghosts," said Violet.

"We'll get to the bottom of it," Benny said. "Right, Henry?"

"I hope so," said Henry. "I'm just not sure how."

CHAPTER 4

In the Spotlight

It was after midnight when Benny awoke to the sound of thunder. He slid out of bed and tiptoed across the room to shut the window. As he peered out into the rainy night, something caught his eye. Was that the beam of a flashlight sweeping back and forth across the backyard?

Henry stirred. "Benny?" he asked sleepily. "What's going on?"

"Somebody's out there," Benny answered in a hushed voice.

Henry came up behind him. "Your eyes must be sharper than mine," he said. "I can't see anybody."

Benny looked at his brother. "Someone just went into the shed."

"I doubt there's anyone out there, Benny."

"But I saw something moving, Henry."

Henry put an arm around his brother. "It's easy to imagine all kinds of things on a dark and stormy night."

Benny shivered in his pajamas. "Don't you think—"

"I think we should get back into our warm beds," said Henry.

Benny nodded. But he knew he had seen someone.

***

"Ray says putting up posters is hard work," Benny said the next morning. He was cracking eggs into a bowl. "We'll need a big breakfast."

"Well, you do have a big appetite, Benny," teased Henry, who was keeping an eye on the bacon sizzling on the stove.

"Something sure smells good," Aunt Jane said, as she came into the kitchen.

"We're making breakfast." Jessie placed a platter of toast on the table. "We wanted to surprise you, Aunt Jane."

"Speaking of surprises," said Henry, "we forgot all about Alice's appointment book."

"Alice's what?" asked Aunt Jane.

"Ray came across Alice's appointment book in the shed," Jessie explained as Henry raced outside. "He thought you should have it as a keepsake."

Henry was back in a flash, waving the appointment book in the air. While he was removing his muddy shoes, Violet noticed something slip from the pages and flutter to the floor. She hurried to pick it up.

"Looks like an ad torn from a newspaper," she said.

"Oh?" Aunt Jane raised an eyebrow. "What does it say, Violet?"

Violet read the ad aloud: *Typist available. Reasonable rates. Ask for Patty at 894-8884.*

Aunt Jane nodded. "Patty must be the college student Alice hired."

"To type the plays she recorded, right?" said Benny.

"Exactly!" said Aunt Jane, surprised that Benny knew this.

"You're mentioned in here a lot," Henry told his aunt, handing her the appointment book. "At least, that's what Ray says."

"Alice and I often got together for a cup of tea." Aunt Jane smiled a little. "She always had a pot of yellow marigolds on the table. Alice loved yellow marigolds, you know. She was always putting them in her plays."

"Lady Chadwick loves marigolds too," said Benny.

"What do you mean?" Aunt Jane asked.

"Remember the hat they found hanging from the chandelier?" said Benny. "Lady Chadwick's hat, I mean. Fern said it had yellow marigolds on it."

"Hmm." Aunt Jane was only half-listening. She was busy leafing through the appointment book.

"Know what else, Aunt Jane?" Benny went on, as he swallowed a mouthful of eggs. "Alice got a new pair of shoes, but they didn't fit. She wanted PJ to take them back. Whoever that is."

"I thought I knew all of Alice's friends." Aunt Jane frowned. "I don't recall anyone with those initials." Putting the appointment book aside, she looked around at the children. "I guess you've got a busy day planned," she added, changing the subject.

Jessie nodded. "I can't wait to see the inside of the theater."

"The whole town's curious to see it," Aunt Jane said. "All the seats have sold out."

"That's great!" said Violet. "I knew everything would work out."

"The play runs all summer, Violet," Aunt Jane reminded her. "We can't be sure tickets will keep selling."

"One thing I don't understand," said Henry. "Even if they don't sell a lot of tickets, why would they close the theater down? It doesn't make sense when they just fixed it up."

"It costs a lot of money to produce plays," Aunt Jane explained. "The town can't afford to keep the theater going if tickets don't sell."

Benny, who was spreading honey on his toast, looked up. "Well, tickets won't sell if Fern quits."

Aunt Jane agreed. "Fern's a wonderful actress," she said. "It would be a disaster if she walks out on the play."

Violet frowned. "You don't think that's possible, do you, Aunt Jane?"

"There's no telling what Fern might do," Aunt Jane replied. "Especially if she thinks the theater's haunted."

"I wish we could do something to help," said Violet.

Aunt Jane smiled. "Putting posters up around town is a big help."

The children quickly finished breakfast, then set off for town on the bikes that Aunt Jane kept for them. When they reached the theater, Jessie noticed something different.

"Looks like Fern got her wish," she said, pointing to the billboard.

The others looked up at the sign. Fern's name now appeared above the title of the play.

"Wow," said Benny. "I guess Ray really wants to keep her happy."

After leaving their bikes behind the theater, the Aldens made their way around to the front.

"I hope I didn't keep you waiting," Ray called out, as he hurried toward them. "I was having breakfast at the diner—with a reporter from the local paper."

"No problem," Henry said, as the director unlocked the theater door. "We just got here ourselves."

As they stepped inside, the children glanced admiringly at the fancy lobby with its red carpeting. Huge mirrors in gold frames covered the walls and a crystal chandelier hung from the ceiling.

"Ooh!" cried Violet. "How beautiful!"

"Is that where you found Lady Chadwick's hat?" Benny pointed up at the light.

Ray nodded. "It still baffles me how it got up there."

"It sure is weird," said Jessie, as they followed the director to the far end of the lobby.

As Ray opened the oak doors that led into the auditorium, he suddenly took a step back in surprise. "What in the world?" he cried. "Somebody's been tampering with the lights."

Sure enough, a large standing spotlight was shining directly onto a seat in the first row of the theater! The Aldens could hardly believe their eyes.

Ray clicked his tongue. "Wait here, kids. I'll only be a minute."

As the director hurried backstage, Jessie said, "I wonder why the spotlight's pointed at the first row?"

"Let's check it out," Henry suggested. He headed down the aisle, the others close behind.

At the front of the theater, Benny's eyes widened. The others followed his gaze to where the circle of yellow light was shining on a seat in the front row—a seat that was littered with popcorn!

"Oh!" Violet's hand flew to her mouth.

"Alice has been here again," Benny said in a hushed voice.

Henry put a comforting arm around his little brother. "Anyone could've done this, Benny."

"Whoever it was," said Jessie, "they wanted everybody to notice."

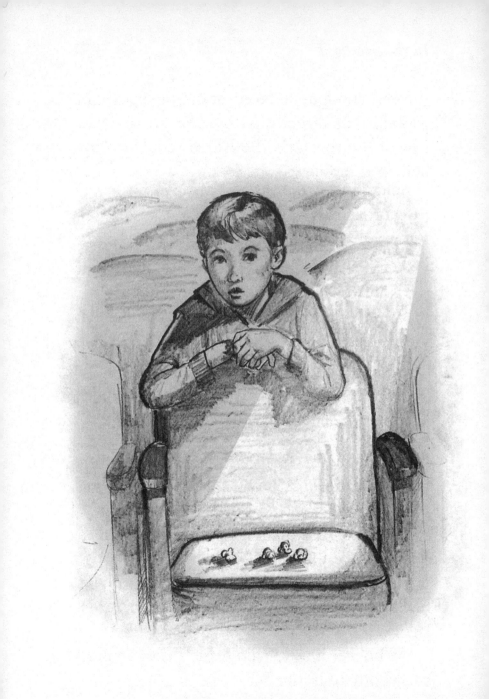

Violet nodded. "They shone the spotlight right on to the seat."

"Let's clean this up before anybody else sees it," Jessie suggested.

Henry agreed. "Fern's nervous enough already."

With that, the Aldens set to work. They found a broom, swept up the popcorn, and threw it into a trash can. They were just finishing when they noticed someone standing close by. An attractive young woman with sandy-colored hair was watching them through narrowed eyes.

"Who are you?" she demanded. "And how'd you get in here?"

The children were so surprised by the woman's harsh tone, they were speechless. Finally, Henry recovered his voice. "We're the Aldens," he said with a friendly smile. "I'm Henry. This is my brother, Benny, and my sisters, Violet and Jessie."

"We're putting posters up around town," Jessie added.

The young woman frowned. "The theater's off-limits to anyone but the cast and crew."

"But we're here to help," protested Benny.

"The last thing we need is a bunch of kids running around," the woman said. "This isn't a playground."

"That's true," said Jessie, who refused to be rude. "And we'll try not to bother you."

"Tricia!" Ray walked over, the rolled up posters tucked under his arm. "What are you doing here so early? Rehearsal isn't for a few hours."

"I know," said Tricia. "But I was driving by and noticed the billboard out front. What's going on, Ray?"

Ray shifted uncomfortably. "Listen, Tricia—"

"No, you listen, Ray!" she cut in. "It's bad enough my name's not even up there, but now *Fern's* name is above the title of my play?"

"Try to understand, Tricia," said Ray. "I'm just trying to keep Fern happy so she won't walk out."

"Who cares if she walks out?" demanded Tricia. "The understudy can play the part of Lady Chadwick, can't she?"

Benny whispered to Henry, "What's an—"

But Henry knew the question before he asked it. "And understudy is somebody who goes on stage if an actor gets sick."

"Or quits," added Jessie.

"Fern wouldn't even have a role if it wasn't for me," Tricia was saying to Ray, her hands on her hips. "First she gets a bigger dressing room, then—"

Ray cut in. "That's enough, Tricia." His mouth was set in a thin, hard line. "I won't have you questioning my decisions."

With that, Tricia turned around and stomped out of the theater.

"Tricia's the winner of the playwriting contest," Ray explained to the children. "I'm afraid her nerves are a bit on edge. She's worried about opening night." He handed the posters to Henry. "There's more posters backstage, but these should keep you busy most of the day."

"We'll come back tomorrow and put up the rest," Jessie offered.

Ray looked surprised. "Are you sure you don't mind?"

The Aldens didn't mind at all. They were happy to do whatever they could to help.

"By the way," Ray added, as the children turned to go, "there's a tape recorder in the box with Alice's tapes. Would you mind bringing it along with you tomorrow? I promised Fern she could use it to practice her lines."

"No problem," said Jessie.

When they were outside the theater, Henry said, "Someone's working hard to make everyone believe there are ghosts in the theater."

"Why anyone would do such a thing?" Jessie wondered.

"You don't think—" Benny began.

"Are you wondering if the theater really is haunted?" Violet asked her little brother. "I don't blame you, Benny. I've been wondering that myself."

Henry shook his head. "A ghost didn't spill that popcorn."

"Now that I think about it," said Violet, "I'm sure there are no ghosts." She wasn't really sure, but she wanted Benny to believe she was.

All morning long the Aldens walked along the streets of Elmford, hanging posters up here, there, and everywhere. Finally, Benny plopped down on a park bench.

"Is it lunchtime yet?" he asked with a sigh.

Henry glanced at his watch. "Close enough," he said. "We could use a break."

Soon enough, the Aldens were sitting down to lunch at the local diner, studying the menus. When the waitress came over, Henry ordered a grilled cheese sandwich and a cola. Jessie had chicken on a bun, coleslaw and milk, and Violet ordered a toasted tomato sandwich and lemonade. Benny decided on a cheeseburger, fries, and chocolate milk.

While they waited for their food to arrive, the children turned their attention to the mystery. "Whoever is behind these pranks," said Jessie, "he—or she—sure knows a lot about Alice Duncan."

"That's true." Violet handed everyone a napkin from the shiny dispenser. "They know that Alice took her knitting and a bag of popcorn to the theater with her."

"And that she sat in the first row," added Benny.

"I'm sure most of Elmford knows that about Alice," said Henry.

As the waitress brought their food, Benny saw someone he knew. "Isn't that Gil Diggs?"

Sure enough, the owner of the local movie theater was sitting at a table in the corner. He was sipping coffee and talking on a cell phone.

"What choice do I have?" Gil was saying. "My business is going nowhere fast."

"He sure looks upset," Violet said, keeping her voice low.

"Yes, of course the whole thing makes me nervous." Gil was talking loudly now. "But I have to shut it down. That's all there is to it!"

"Uh-oh," whispered Benny. "Is Gil talking about the Trap-Door Theater?"

The Aldens looked at one another. None of them liked the sound of this.

CHAPTER 5

Whodunit?

When the Aldens returned to the theater, they found Ray outside by the back door. He was standing at an old table covered with tools and rags. The container filled with plaster of paris was nearby. He looked over at the children and gave them a cheery smile.

"How did you make out?" he asked them.

"Good," Henry told him. "We found a spot for every poster."

Ray dried his hands on a rag. Then he

reached into his pocket and pulled out some dollar bills. "Let me pay you for—"

Jessie shook her head firmly. "Please put your money away, Ray."

"But..." he protested.

"We like to help," Violet said in her soft voice.

Ray hesitated for a moment. Then he shoved the dollar bills into his pocket again. "If you won't accept money, then at least accept my invitation to the dress rehearsal tomorrow night. We're having a potluck dinner for the cast and crew afterward. I'd love to have you and your aunt join us."

"We'll check with Aunt Jane," said Jessie. "But I'm pretty sure you can count us in."

"I hope so," said Ray, turning back to his work.

Benny was curious. "What are you making, Ray?"

"I'm making that mold of the butler's footprint, Benny. The stagehands are busy backstage, so I thought I'd do it myself."

"Super!" said Benny.

"I already made an impression of the

butler's shoe in the mud." Ray nodded toward a square container filled with dirt. "It's important to make the mold before the mud dries."

"Why's that?" Henry wondered.

"A footprint shrinks as the mud dries, Henry," Ray explained. "For the mold to fit the butler's shoe exactly, it has to be made while the dirt's still wet."

"That makes sense," said Henry.

The Aldens watched as the theater director stirred the plaster of paris with water. When it was just the right thickness, he poured the mixture into the footprint.

"That should do it. Hopefully, the ghosts won't get at it before the plaster sets," Ray said with a wink.

Jessie caught Henry's eye. Was Ray joking—or did he really believe the theater was haunted?

***

"Let's get that tape recorder for Ray before we forget," Jessie suggested, as they wheeled their bikes into Aunt Jane's driveway.

"Good idea," said Henry.

"Ray said it was in the box with Alice's tapes," Benny reminded them, following the others into the shed.

"That's funny," Violet said, looking around. "I'm sure it was right here on the table." Now there was nothing on the table but the old typewriter.

"I don't understand it," said Henry.

Jessie frowned. "What happened?"

"It was stolen," said Benny.

"Oh, Benny," said Jessie. "Who would steal Alice Duncan's tapes?"

"A thief, that's who!" Benny cried.

Henry looked over at his little brother. "You're thinking about last night, right?"

"I saw somebody out by the shed, Henry," Benny insisted. "I'm sure of it."

Jessie and Violet were surprised to hear this.

"But who would do such a thing?" Violet wondered. "And why?"

"Let's not say anything about the tapes," Henry suggested, "until we have a chance to do some investigating."

Over dinner, the Aldens took turns telling

their aunt all about the latest prank. Violet finished by saying, "A spotlight was shining on a seat in the first row."

"I can't believe it!" Aunt Jane shook her head. "Those practical jokes won't seem very funny if they scare people away."

"Don't worry, Aunt Jane," said Benny. "We cleaned up the popcorn before anybody else could see it."

"That was good thinking, Benny," Aunt Jane told him, as she pushed her chair back.

"We'll do the dishes, Aunt Jane," Violet offered.

"Oh, thanks, Violet. It'll give me a chance to get some other work done." With that, Aunt Jane left the room.

"Maybe if we put our heads together," Jessie said, as she wrapped the leftover pasta, "we can get to the bottom of it."

But Violet wasn't so sure. "This is a tough mystery to figure out."

"Know what?" said Benny. "I think Alice's tapes will show up again—in a strange place."

"What makes you say that?" Jessie asked her little brother.

"Remember what happened when Lady Chadwick's hat disappeared?" Benny reminded them. "They found it hanging from the chandelier in the lobby!"

Violet, who was filling the sink with soapy water, suddenly looked over. "You think the disappearing tapes is just another prank?"

"It's possible," Henry said thoughtfully.

Benny had an opinion about this. "I bet it is a trick," he said. "And I bet Gil Diggs is behind it."

"Gil's up to something, all right," said Henry. "I'm just not sure it has anything to do with the ghostly pranks."

"But we heard him on the phone," Benny argued. "Remember? He was talking about shutting it down."

"And the Trap-Door Theater *will* shut down," Violet pointed out, "if everybody's scared away by rumors of ghosts."

"You're forgetting something," Jessie said. "Gil doesn't have a key to the theater."

"That's true," said Henry. "Ray told us he has the only key."

"And he said there was no sign anyone

broke in," Violet recalled.

"What if Gil is working with someone else?" Jessie suggested.

Henry hadn't thought of that. "There was somebody on the other end of that phone conversation," he admitted. "Maybe Gil knows somebody in the cast."

"Or the crew," added Benny.

Henry reached for a dish towel. "Gil is afraid the Trap-Door Theater will take away even more customers," he admitted. "But he's not the only suspect."

"You're thinking about Tricia Jenkins, right?" said Jessie.

Benny looked puzzled. "Why would Tricia play tricks on everyone?"

"There's no reason for her to do something like that," said Violet.

"What if she's trying to get rid of Fern Robson?" Henry suggested.

"By convincing her the theater's haunted?" asked Violet.

"We have to think of everything," Henry pointed out. "And Tricia doesn't seem to like Fern very much."

"She didn't seem very happy to see Fern's name on the billboard above the title," Jessie had to admit.

"It's not very nice to scare people." A frown crossed Benny's round face.

"No, it's not," agreed Violet, who was up to her elbows in soapy suds. "Fern's a nervous wreck."

"Maybe that's just what she wants everyone to believe," Jessie said. "Maybe she isn't nervous at all."

Henry turned to Jessie in surprise. "You think it's an act?"

"Could be," Jessie said, putting the clean plates into the cupboard. "It does seem to get her what she wants."

Henry added everything up on his fingers. "First she gets a bigger dressing room. Then she gets to sleep in late."

"And don't forget about getting her name above the title," put in Jessie.

They had to admit it was possible. After all, Fern was an actress—and a good one. And wasn't Ray eager to keep her happy so she wouldn't quit?

"You really think Fern set up all those pranks just to get her own way?" Violet found it hard to believe.

Jessie shrugged. "Well, she seems to be able to wrap Ray around her little finger by acting frightened."

"It does seem that way," Violet said. But she didn't like to think Fern would do something so sneaky.

"Let's keep an eye on all of them," Henry suggested. "Gil, Tricia, and Fern."

Jessie suddenly looked around. "Where's Benny?"

Henry looked around too. "I don't know."

A few minutes later, Benny came in from the backyard. There was a smudge of dirt on his nose.

"Where were you, Benny?" Jessie wanted to know.

"I was on a top secret mission," Benny said mysteriously. "But I can't tell you about it just yet."

The other Aldens looked at one other. What was their little brother up to?

CHAPTER 6

Uh-oh!

When the Aldens came downstairs the next morning, a pancake breakfast was waiting for them. Aunt Jane was having a cup of coffee and reading the paper. She looked up as the children came into the room.

"You're not going to believe what's in the paper," she said, shaking her head.

The Aldens were instantly curious. As they crowded around, Aunt Jane read the headline aloud: Is THE TRAP-DOOR THEATER HAUNTED?

"Oh, no!" Violet cried.

Over breakfast, Aunt Jane read the article to them. It was all about the strange things that had been happening at the theater. It finished with the story of the spilled popcorn—and the spotlight shining on the first row.

"I don't get it." Henry lifted a sausage onto his plate. "We cleared all the popcorn away before anybody saw it. How did the newspaper find out?"

"I suppose somebody leaked it to them," said Aunt Jane.

"But we were the only ones who knew about it," Benny insisted, pouring syrup over his stack of pancakes.

"You're forgetting about Ray," Henry reminded them.

"Oh, right." Benny licked a drop of syrup from the back of his hand.

"You think Ray told the paper?" Violet wondered.

Henry nodded. "That'd be my guess. After all, he said they wouldn't do a write-up on the theater—unless it was sure to grab the readers' attention."

"But...will people still will buy tickets?" Benny wanted to know.

Aunt Jane sighed. "It could go either way."

"Either way?" Benny repeated, not understanding.

"The Trap-Door Theater just made front-page news," said Aunt Jane.

Henry understood what she meant. "Some people might think this is good publicity."

Aunt Jane nodded. "Only time will tell if it brings folks into the theater or—"

"Scares them away," finished Violet.

Everyone was unusually quiet as they ate breakfast. They were lost in thought about the mystery. It wasn't until they stepped outside that Benny spoke up.

"Come on!" he said, breaking into a run. "Come and see what I made."

Henry, Jessie, and Violet hurried across the yard behind Benny. They came to a stop outside the shed.

"It's a mold of the prowler's footprint," Benny told them proudly.

Sure enough, a shoe print in the dirt had been filled with plaster.

"So that's what you were up to yesterday!" Jessie realized.

Benny nodded, beaming. "Now we can figure out who stole the box of tapes."

"That's good detective work, Benny," Henry said, taking a closer look at the mold. "There's only one problem...a prowler didn't make this footprint."

"How can you be sure?" Jessie asked.

Henry pulled off his sneaker. "Take a look at the tread on the bottom of my shoe."

"Oh!" cried Violet. "It matches the markings in the plaster."

Benny's jaw dropped. "But..."

"I stepped in the mud yesterday," Henry explained, "when I came out to get Alice's appointment book for Aunt Jane."

"That can't be your shoe print, Henry," Benny insisted. "See? The mold's too small for your shoe."

"Benny's right," Violet said.

"There's a reason for that," Henry said. "The footprint was made when the ground was still wet from the rain. Remember what Ray told us? A footprint shrinks when the sun dries up the mud."

"Oh, right. And Benny made the mold after the sun had been out all day," Jessie realized.

Benny's shoulders slumped. He looked crushed. Violet felt her little brother's disappointment. "Never mind," she said, as they walked their bikes across the yard. "It was a good try."

"It sure was," agreed Jessie. "Nobody else even thought of looking for footprints."

Benny brightened. "Good detectives always think of stuff like that."

"Come on, Benny," Henry said, giving his brother a playful nudge. "We've got posters to put up." With that, the four Aldens pedaled away.

When they arrived at the Trap-Door Theater, they spotted Ray giving directions to the crew on stage. As the children came down the aisle, the director looked up and gave them a friendly wave.

"Be right with you, kids!" he called out. "Why don't you take a seat for a minute?"

"Ray won't be very happy when he finds

out about the missing tape recorder," Henry said, as they sat down in the front row.

"And the missing tapes," added Jessie.

Benny, who was bending over to tie up his shoe, suddenly said, "That's funny."

"What's is it, Benny?" Jessie asked.

"There's something under my seat." The others looked over as Benny pulled out a wooden box.

"Is that what I think it is?" Violet asked in disbelief.

As Benny lifted the lid, they all stared wide-eyed at Alice's tapes.

"Look," said Jessie. "The tape recorder's in there too."

"Uh-oh!" Benny's eyes were huge. "I bet I'm sitting in Alice Duncan's seat!"

Just then, Ray hurried over with the posters. "Sorry to keep you waiting. These are the last of the posters." He looked surprised when he spotted the tapes on Benny's lap. "I see you brought the whole box with you. Actually, I only needed the tape recorder."

"We didn't bring the box with us, Ray,"

Jessie said, handing him the tape recorder as he handed her the posters. "Somebody stole the tapes from Aunt Jane's shed."

Ray looked confused. "Isn't that the box of tapes on Benny's lap?"

"Yes," said Henry. "But Benny just found it."

"What?" Ray laughed a little. "You're kidding, right?"

"It was under my seat," Benny told him.

"But…how did that happen?" asked Ray.

Henry shrugged. "I guess it's another practical joke."

Ray stared at the box of tapes. Then he turned on his heel and quickly walked away.

"That was odd," said Violet. "It's just another prank, right? I wonder why Ray looked so shocked."

Benny shrugged. "It doesn't make sense."

"Nothing about this mystery makes sense," said Henry.

Nobody could argue with that.

CHAPTER 7

A Shrinking Footprint

At the dress rehearsal that evening, the Aldens sat in the audience with Aunt Jane and Ray Shaw. The play was full of suspense— the children watched as Lady Chadwick tracked down clues to find the thief of a priceless diamond necklace. In the final act, with all the suspects gathered together, Lady Chadwick summed up the case. "I came across a footprint in the dried mud," she said. "After making a plaster mold of the print, I soon discovered it fit someone's shoe exactly. In fact, the thief is in this very room. I believe the butler did it!"

The Aldens suddenly looked at one another in surprise. "Did you hear that?" whispered Benny.

"Yes," Jessie whispered back. "There's a mistake in the play!"

Henry nodded. "If Lady Chadwick made the mold when the mud was dry—"

"The footprint would've shrunk!" finished Violet.

Jessie agreed. "It would never fit the butler's shoe exactly."

As the curtain went down, Aunt Jane turned to the director. "What a wonderful play!" she said, clapping along with the children. Ray looked pleased. "I just hope it goes half as well on opening night."

Backstage, they found everyone gathered together in one of the dressing rooms. The cast and crew were helping themselves to the hot and cold food set out on a long table. The children followed the line of people slowly around the table while Aunt Jane went over to congratulate Fern Robson.

After helping themselves to the different dishes, the Aldens sat down in a corner with their heaping plates. "Did you get some of Aunt Jane's sweet-and-sour meatballs, Benny?" Violet asked. "They're really good."

Benny nodded as he crunched into a pickle. "Should we tell Ray?" he asked. "About the footprint, I mean."

"Let's hold off on that for now," Jessie suggested, as she looked around at all the smiling faces.

Henry was quick to agree. "Everybody's having such a good time. It'd be a shame to spoil it."

Just then, something caught Violet's eye. "Don't all look at once," she said, "but isn't that Gil Diggs talking to Ray?"

One by one, the other Aldens looked over. "That's Gil, all right," Jessie said in surprise. "I wonder what he's doing here?"

"Beats me," said Henry. "He's not exactly a big fan of the Trap-Door Theater."

A moment later, Aunt Jane sat down beside Benny. "I was just having a chat with Gil," she said. "Guess what he told me?"

The children were instantly curious. "What was it, Aunt Jane?"

"He's planning to turn his movie theater into a children's playhouse!"

Benny's eyebrows shot up. "A playhouse?" he echoed. "You mean, like our boxcar?"

Aunt Jane smiled a little. "Not exactly, Benny. Instead of showing movies in his theater, he'll be putting on plays for children."

"That's not a bad idea," Henry said, thoughtfully.

"Gil stopped by to get some pointers from Ray," Aunt Jane explained. "Apparently, he got a loan from the bank. Of course," she added, "it'll mean shutting his theater down for a while to build a stage. But Gil thinks it'll be worth it."

Jessie suddenly understood. *That's* what Gil had meant on the phone: he was talking about shutting down his own theater!

The Aldens looked at one another. They were each thinking the same thing. They could cross Gil Diggs off their list of suspects.

"Ah, there you are, Jane!" Ray hurried over with Tricia Jenkins. "I wanted to introduce you to our contest winner."

Aunt Jane held out her hand. "So nice to meet you, Tricia. I don't know when I've enjoyed a play more," she said with a warm smile. "By the way, do you know the children? This is Henry and—"

"We've met," Tricia broke in, barely looking over.

Jessie and Henry exchanged glances. It was clear Tricia wasn't pleased to see them again.

"That surprise twist in the last act was brilliant," Aunt Jane went on. "I never saw it coming!"

Ray nodded approvingly. "Tricia has a real gift for keeping an audience on the edge of their seats. Right, Fern?" he added, as the actress joined their group.

"Yes, it's a wonderful play," Fern agreed, looking over at the author. "One thing, though, Tricia. I always try to understand the character I'm playing. Maybe you could shed some light on Lady Chadwick's hat."

Tricia blinked in surprise. "What are you talking about?"

"I'm talking about the flowers," said Fern.

"It must mean something that Lady Chadwick wears them on her hat."

"It means she likes carnations." Tricia shrugged. "It's as simple as that."

"You mean marigolds," Fern said. "Those are yellow marigolds on her hat."

"No, they're carnations, aren't they?" Tricia argued.

"Marigolds," Fern said, shaking her head.

"Well...whatever," said Tricia, shrugging.

"I'm surprised at you, Tricia," Fern told her. "You underlined 'yellow marigolds' in your script. How could you forget?"

"Honestly, Fern!" Tricia snapped. "Why do you have to make such a big deal out of everything? Lady Chadwick is fond of yellow marigolds. End of story."

Jessie caught Henry's eye. Why was Tricia getting so upset?

"Alice Duncan liked them too," Benny was saying. "Yellow marigolds, I mean."

Tricia seemed startled by Benny's remark. "I'm afraid I wouldn't know about that," she said, fiddling nervously with her necklace. "I never had the pleasure of meeting Alice Duncan."

Violet couldn't help noticing the gold heart on the chain around Tricia's neck. The heart was engraved with the letters *PJ*. Something seemed oddly familiar about the initials. But Violet couldn't quite put her finger on what it was.

"Well, I think Alice would be very pleased if she knew yellow marigolds appeared in the winning play," Aunt Jane remarked. "They were her favorite flower."

Ray chuckled. "Alice was quite a character, wasn't she? And how about that old typewriter of hers? Now, there's a real antique!"

Aunt Jane nodded. "The keys kept sticking, but that never stopped Alice."

"I prefer a computer, myself," Tricia said, her voice cold. "I can't imagine using an old typewriter that doesn't print *w* at all." With that, she turned and walked away.

Jessie stared after her, puzzled. Nobody had mentioned the typewriter wouldn't print *w*. How did Tricia know?

Chapter 8

Something Smells Fishy

"We should tell Ray about the footprint," Benny insisted, as they worked in Aunt Jane's vegetable garden the next day.

"I think so too," said Jessie, shaking the dirt from the roots of a weed. Henry nodded. "We'll tell Ray about it the next time we see him."

"I'm sure it'd be easy enough to change the script," Violet added.

Henry sat down on a rock. "Wow, that afternoon sun sure is getting hot," he said. "I vote we cool off in the pond."

"I second that!" said Jessie. "Let's clean up here, then we can change into our swim suits."

As they put the garden tools away in the shed, Henry noticed that Jessie's gaze was fixed on the old typewriter.

"What is it, Jessie?" he asked.

"I was just wondering how Tricia knew about Alice's typewriter," she said. "That it wouldn't print *w* at all, I mean. I'm sure no one mentioned it."

Henry, Violet, and Benny had thought nothing of it. But now they wondered about it too.

"That is weird," said Violet.

Jessie nodded. "Tricia must have met Alice."

"Do you think she told a lie?" Benny wanted to know.

"I doubt it," said Henry, "and I'll tell you why. If she had been a friend of Alice's, Aunt Jane would have met her before last night."

"Good point," said Jessie, as they stepped outside. "Aunt Jane said she knew all of Alice's friends."

"Not all," Benny argued. "Aunt Jane didn't know PJ."

"Who?" Jessie looked puzzled, but only for a moment. "Oh, you mean the friend in Alice's appointment book."

Violet suddenly whirled around. "That's it!"

"What's it?" Benny wanted to know.

"I knew there was something familiar about the initials on Tricia's necklace," Violet explained, her voice rising with excitement. "The letters *p* and *j* were engraved on the gold heart she was wearing."

Benny scratched his head. "But...Tricia's name begins with a *t*, doesn't it?"

"Yes, but Patricia starts with a *p*," Violet pointed out.

"Oh, I get it!" cried Benny, catching on. "Tricia is short for Patricia."

Violet nodded. "I have a hunch Tricia is PJ."

"If you're right, Violet," said Jessie, "then Tricia really did lie about not knowing Alice."

Benny frowned. "I wonder why she'd do something like that?"

"Beats me!" Henry shrugged. "I think I'm too hot to think straight right now."

With that, they hurried off to change into their swim suits. For a while, they put all thoughts of the mystery aside as they splashed about in the pond near their aunt's house. It wasn't until they were heading back across the clover fields, towels flung over their shoulders, that Jessie suddenly snapped her fingers.

"Tricia isn't the only nickname for Patricia!" she cried.

Henry stopped. "What are you talking about, Jessie?"

"Remember that ad for a typist? The one that fell out of Alice's appointment book."

Henry nodded. So did Violet and Benny.

"What was the name in the ad?" Jessie asked.

Henry thought for a moment. "Wasn't it Patty?"

"Exactly," said Jessie. "And Patty is another nickname for—"

"Patricia!" cried Violet, in sudden understanding.

This got Henry thinking. "Tricia *did* change her nickname," he recalled. "At least, that's what Ray said."

"Maybe she thought Tricia had more pizzazz than Patty," guessed Benny.

"Wait a minute," said Violet. "Are you saying it was Tricia's ad in the paper?"

"I'm not a hundred percent sure," Jessie answered. "But it's possible Tricia and Patty are the same person."

"Then that would mean Alice hired Tricia to type up her plays," Henry concluded.

They had to admit it was possible. Didn't Aunt Jane say that Alice hired a college student? And didn't Tricia earn money for school on her computer?

"I don't get it." Benny frowned. "Why would Tricia lie about it?"

"That's a good question, Benny," said Henry.

"We can't be sure Tricia and Patty are the same person," Violet pointed out.

"You're right," Jessie was forced to admit.

"I guess there's no way of proving it," added Henry.

"I know a way," cried Benny, racing ahead. He called back over his shoulder, "Come on!"

As soon as they got back to the house, the youngest Alden headed straight for Alice's appointment book. When he gave it a shake, the ad fell out onto the kitchen table.

"What's up?" Henry asked, trying to catch his breath.

Benny handed him the newspaper clipping. "I think we should call this number."

Henry slapped his brother a high five. "You're a genius!"

Benny grinned. "I guess I am."

Jessie, Violet, and Benny gathered around as Henry dialed the number in the ad. He held the receiver up so they could all listen. With their heads close together, they heard the message on the answering machine: "Hi, you've reached Patty. Please leave a message and I'll return your call as soon as possible."

"There's no doubt about it," Jessie said, as Henry hung up. "That was Tricia's voice."

"This is getting stranger and stranger," said Benny.

"It sure is." Violet poured lemonade into four tall glasses. "If Tricia was hired to type

Alice's plays, why would she keep it a secret? There's nothing wrong with helping Alice, is there?"

"No," said Henry. "Not if that's all it was."

"You think there's more to it than that?" Violet wondered.

"Got to be." Henry sounded very sure. "Why else would Tricia want to keep it a secret?"

Nobody said anything for a while. They were all deep in thought as they sat around the kitchen table, sipping lemonade.

"It does seem strange," Jessie said at last. "It's almost as if Tricia's hiding something."

"That's not all that's strange," said Henry, who was staring at the last entry in Alice's appointment book.

Benny was swirling the ice cubes in his glass. "What is it, Henry?" he asked.

"There's something weird about this last entry."

"What's weird about it, Henry?" Benny wanted to know. "Alice bought shoes that didn't fit. You said that yourself the other day."

"I said that then. Now I'm not so sure."

"What are you thinking, Henry?" Violet wondered.

"Alice didn't write 'shoes won't fit'—she wrote '*shoe* won't fit.'"

Jessie inched her chair closer. "You're right," she said, glancing at the appointment book. "It *does* say shoe—not shoes." She looked from Henry to the entry and back again. "That is a bit weird."

Henry said, "Maybe this entry has nothing to do with returning a pair of shoes."

"What else could it mean?" Violet wanted to know.

Henry paused for a moment to sort out his thoughts. "What if Alice was talking about the butler's shoe?"

Benny blinked in surprise. "Alice had a butler?"

"No, no." Henry smiled a little at this. "I'm talking about Lady Chadwick's butler."

"What are you saying, Henry?" Jessie asked.

"What if Alice noticed the mistake in the play?" said Henry. "Maybe she realized the butler's shoe wouldn't fit a mold that was made in dried mud."

"You think Alice wanted PJ—Tricia—to make a change to the script?" Violet asked, after a moment's thought.

"I'm only guessing," said Henry. "But I think it's possible."

"If you're right," Jessie concluded, "then Alice must've read Tricia's play."

Violet thought about this. "Maybe Alice was giving her a few pointers."

"Could be," said Henry. "But why would Tricia keep it a secret? That's the part I don't get."

Violet nodded. "There's something here we're not understanding."

"I don't know what to make of it either," said Jessie. "Unless..."

"Unless what?" asked Benny.

Jessie's mind was racing. "I keep thinking about Lady Chadwick's hat."

"That it was hanging from the chandelier in the lobby?" said Benny. "Is that what you mean, Jessie?"

"No, it's not that."

"What then?" asked Henry.

"I'm talking about the yellow marigolds,"

said Jessie. "Don't you think it's odd Tricia didn't remember what kind of flowers Lady Chadwick was wearing?"

Benny nodded. "She called them carnations."

"Exactly," said Jessie. "And yet, she underlined 'yellow marigolds' in the script. At least, that's what Fern said."

Henry was curious. "Where are you going with this, Jessie?"

"Yellow marigolds were Alice's favorite flower," Jessie reminded them, hoping they would understand what she was driving at. Seeing their puzzled faces, she added, "Alice always put yellow marigolds in her plays."

"You think it's more than just a coincidence?" Violet wondered. "That Tricia put yellow marigolds in her play too, I mean."

Jessie nodded her head slowly. "I think it's a lot more than just a coincidence."

"Back up a minute, Jessie," Henry put in. "Are you saying Alice noticed a mistake—in her own play?"

"That's exactly what I'm saying," Jessie told him. "It's possible she wanted to make the change before Tricia typed up the last act."

Violet's eyes widened. "You really think Alice Duncan wrote *Lady Chadwick's Riddle?*"

"If she did...that means—" began Benny.

Henry cut in. "It means Tricia put her name on Alice's play."

"Oh!" Violet put her hand over her mouth. "You don't really think Tricia would do something so terrible, do you?"

"I don't want to believe it, Violet," said Jessie. "But it's a pretty strong case against Tricia."

Henry agreed. "It would explain why Tricia lied about knowing Alice."

"And she could easily have put her name on *Lady Chadwick's Riddle* after Alice died," Jessie pointed out.

"But why would Tricia do something like that?" Violet wondered.

Henry shrugged. "Maybe she saw the contest as a way to make some quick cash."

Benny was thinking. "I bet Tricia stole Alice's tapes too."

"You might be on to something, Benny," Henry had to admit. "Chances are, she wanted to make sure there wasn't another copy of Alice's play."

"Still," said Violet, "I don't think we should jump to any conclusions."

Henry nodded. "You're right, Violet. It's one thing to suspect someone. It's another thing to have proof."

"But we can't just do nothing," Benny insisted. "Can we?"

"It wouldn't hurt to ask a few questions," Henry said after a moment's thought. "Aunt Jane has some errands to run in town. Maybe we could get a ride with her to the theater."

The Aldens weren't sure what they were going to do. They only knew they had to do something.

CHAPTER 9

Pointing a Finger

As they pulled up in front of the Trap-Door Theater, Aunt Jane glanced at her watch. "I'll get my errands done, then meet you back here."

"Perfect!" said Henry, as they climbed out of the car.

Aunt Jane gave them a little wave, then drove away.

Violet slowed her step. "What if we're wrong?" She was having second thoughts about their suspicions.

"Grandfather says we're seldom wrong when it comes to hunches," Benny reminded her.

"And if we're right," added Jessie, "we can't let Tricia get away with stealing Alice's play, can we?"

Henry held the theater door open. "Don't worry, Violet," he said. "We'll just ask a few questions and see how Tricia reacts."

"That sounds fair," agreed Violet.

Inside the theater, the Aldens hurried backstage where preparations for opening night were in full swing. Stagehands were rushing about, testing the lights and setting up props. As the children passed an opened door, a familiar voice called out to them.

"The Aldens!"

Ray, who was sitting at his desk, motioned for them to come in. Across from him, Tricia Jenkins and Fern Robson had their heads bent over their scripts.

"Did you forget we're out of posters?" Ray asked, smiling as the children stepped into his office.

"No, we didn't forget," Henry told him.

"We were hoping you might have time to talk. It's about Alice Duncan."

Tricia suddenly glanced up from her script. A look of shock crossed her face, but only for a moment. She quickly pulled herself together. "We're in the middle of a script meeting," she said, making a shooing motion with her hand. "The play opens tomorrow night. We don't have time to chat."

"Speak for yourself." Fern frowned over at Tricia. "I could use a break."

"Let's take five," Ray suggested. He put his feet up on his desk and leaned back with his hands behind his head. "What's up, kids?"

The Aldens looked at one other. They weren't really sure how to begin. Finally, Violet spoke up.

"The thing is," she said in a quiet voice, "we noticed a mistake in the play."

Jessie nodded. "We thought we should mention it."

Tricia looked amused. "Well, aren't we lucky we have the Aldens around to give us a few pointers," she said, though it was clear from her voice that she didn't think they were lucky at all.

Henry squared his shoulders. "It's true," he insisted. "There's a mistake in the last act." He reminded Ray of what he'd told them— that a footprint shrinks after the sun dries up the mud. Henry finished by saying, "If Lady Chadwick made the mold when the mud was dry, the butler's shoe would never fit exactly."

"Of course!" said Ray. "How could I miss that?" He shook his head. "Looks like we'll be making a change to the script."

Tricia stiffened. "No one pays attention to that stuff. Do you honestly think anyone will notice?"

"The Aldens did," Ray reminded her.

"And so did Alice Duncan!" Benny blurted out.

Henry and Jessie exchanged glances. There was no going back now. They could only hope they were on the right track.

"Alice Duncan noticed?" Fern's mouth dropped open. "That's strange."

"Not as strange as you might think," Jessie told her. "You see, Alice made one last entry in her appointment book before she died."

"Yes, I remember seeing it." Ray nodded his head slowly. "Something about returning a pair of shoes, wasn't it?"

"That's what we thought too," said Henry. "At first."

"And now?"

"Now we think Alice realized there was a mistake in the last act of *Lady Chadwick's Riddle*," said Violet. "That's why she wrote, 'Shoe won't fit. Tell PJ to make change.'"

"PJ?" Fern looked over at Tricia suspiciously. "Patricia Jenkins?"

"Hang on a minute!" Ray put up a hand. "How would *Alice* know anything about a mistake in *your* play, Tricia?"

Tricia swallowed hard. Everyone's eyes were fixed on her. Finally, she cleared her throat and said, "Alice Duncan was giving me advice on my play. What's wrong with that?"

"Why would Alice give advice to someone she didn't know?" demanded Henry.

It was a good question. Tricia said she'd never met Alice. Everyone waited expectantly for an answer.

"I never actually met Alice," said Tricia.

"But I did send my play to her in the mail."

The children looked at each another. Tricia seemed to have an answer for everything. But Henry wasn't giving up so easily.

"Are you sure there wasn't more to it than that?" he asked, giving Tricia a meaningful look.

"What are you saying?" Tricia snapped. "You can't prove I've done anything dishonest."

Ray's eyes narrowed as he looked over at Tricia. But he didn't say anything.

"I bet a tape of Alice's play would prove it," Benny said, his hands on his hips.

"What?" Tricia shifted nervously. "But... I...I checked every one of those tapes and—" She stopped abruptly as if realizing she'd said too much.

Henry and Jessie looked at each other in surprise. Benny's remark had only been wishful thinking. Had Tricia misunderstood? Did she think they actually had Alice's voice on tape—recording *Lady Chadwick's Riddle*?

Benny looked Tricia straight in the eye. "You stole the box of tapes from Aunt Jane's shed, didn't you?"

"That's ridiculous!" Tricia forced a tense laugh. "Why would I do something like that?"

Henry spoke up. "You wanted to make sure there wasn't another copy of *Lady Chadwick's Riddle*."

"What's this all about, kids?" asked Ray, who was pacing around the room. "Surely you're not suggesting Tricia stole Alice Duncan's play?"

When she heard this, Fern's jaw dropped. She was too shocked to speak.

"What do you have to say for yourself, Tricia?" Ray asked.

Tricia opened her mouth several times as if about to speak, then closed it again. Finally, she sank back in her chair, looking defeated. "It's true," she confessed, burying her head in her hands. "I signed my name to Alice Duncan's play."

"What?" Ray stopped pacing. "How could you do such a thing?"

"I knew it was wrong," Tricia admitted, "but when I heard about the contest, I decided to enter Alice's play." She lifted her head. "The funny thing is, I really didn't believe

Lady Chadwick's Riddle would win."

Jessie guessed what was coming next. "When it did, you decided to keep the cash."

Tricia didn't deny it. "I've always had to work so hard to put myself through school."

Ray looked at her, stunned. "That doesn't make it okay to steal."

"How did you get hold of Alice's play in the first place?" Fern wanted to know.

Violet turned to Tricia. "Alice hired you to type her plays, didn't she?"

Tricia nodded. "I was finishing up the last act of *Lady Chadwick's Riddle* when Alice died. I figured if I put my name on the play, nobody would ever catch on. I really couldn't see the harm," she added, trying to make light of it. "After all, Alice would finally have a play performed in public."

"And you could take the credit for it," finished Fern.

"And the cash," added Jessie.

"There was only one problem," said Ray. "You hadn't counted on the Aldens coming along and figuring everything out."

Tricia had to admit this was true. "I thought

it was a foolproof plan, Ray. At least, until I overheard you talking about Alice's tape recorder. You said it was in the box with her tapes. That's when it suddenly hit me that Alice might have made an extra copy of her play."

"So you went out to Aunt Jane's on that rainy night," Benny said. "And you took the tapes from the shed. I saw you."

"Yes, I did," Tricia confessed. "I checked every one of those tapes, but I couldn't find another copy of *Lady Chadwick's Riddle*."

"That's because there isn't another copy," Jessie informed her.

"You...you don't really have Alice's voice on tape?" Tricia's shoulders slumped. "I can't believe I fell for your bluff."

"You almost got away with it, Tricia," Ray realized. Then he added, "You left the box of tapes under a seat in the first row, didn't you?"

Tricia nodded. "I figured everyone would think it was just another prank."

"Let me get this straight," said Fern, her eyes flashing. "You're the one who staged all those ghostly pranks?"

"No!" Tricia cried. "I took Alice's tapes, but that's all. I had nothing to do with anything else."

The Aldens exchanged looks. Was Tricia telling the truth?

"I can't believe you took credit for someone else's work," said Ray. "How could you tell such a lie?" He sounded more disappointed than angry.

Tricia looked at the floor. "I wish I could go back and undo what I've done," she said, her voice shaking. "I'm so sorry."

"Sorry isn't enough," Ray told her, his face grim. "You'll have to return the prize money, Tricia. And it'll be a long time before anyone will trust you again."

With that, Tricia walked slowly from the room, looking truly regretful.

Chapter 10

Taking a Bow

"I just can't believe it," Ray told Aunt Jane and the Aldens on opening night. They were gathered in Fern's dressing room during intermission. "Tickets have been selling like hotcakes!"

"Isn't it wonderful?" said Fern, who was sitting at her dressing table. "The play's sold out right through the summer!" She pulled out a tissue and blotted her lipstick.

Violet's eyes were shining. "That's great news!"

"When the truth came out about Tricia Jenkins," said Ray, "I was afraid nobody would come near the theater."

"That worried me too." Aunt Jane nodded. "But, thank goodness, the newspaper put a great spin on everything."

The Aldens grinned as Henry pointed to the headline: Two MYSTERIES FOR THE PRICE OF ONE!

The report described how Tricia tried to steal Alice Duncan's play—and how the Aldens had pieced together clues and cracked the case.

Fern powdered her nose. "That article really caught the public's interest."

But the children knew the mystery wasn't fully explained. They still weren't sure who was behind all the ghostly pranks at the theater.

Henry had a question. "There's something I don't understand, Fern. If you really believed the theater was haunted, why did you keep coming here?"

"Oh, it wasn't easy, Henry," Fern told him. "I even broke out in a nervous rash. See?"

She pushed up her sleeve. "But you know what they say—the show must go on!"

Henry looked at Jessie. Jessie nodded. Fern really believed the theater was haunted. It wasn't just an act.

"I knew you wouldn't let everyone down, Fern," said Ray. "And you must admit, we sure got some good publicity out of those ghostly pranks."

"Is that why you told the newspaper about the popcorn, Ray?" asked Henry.

"Yes." Ray nodded. "When I met the reporter—that morning at the diner—I told him everything. I figured I'd give him something worth writing about. I didn't want the article buried somewhere in the back pages. And it did the trick too," he added proudly. "That story made front-page news."

Benny, who had been listening with a puzzled frown, suddenly spoke up. "But you met with the reporter before we even saw the spilled popcorn."

The Aldens looked at each other. Something didn't add up. How could Ray mention something he hadn't even seen?

"Well, I, um…" Ray struggled to find something to say. Then he took a deep breath and said, "I guess you found me out."

"What are you saying, Ray?" Aunt Jane looked puzzled.

"I'm saying I was behind all those practical jokes."

"What?" Fern stared at the director. She paused as if she couldn't quite believe what she had heard. "You tried to scare me?"

"It's not what you think, Fern," Ray told her. "I never meant to scare you. I even made sure you wouldn't be at the theater to see the spilled popcorn."

"That's why you wanted Fern to get her beauty sleep that morning," guessed Jessie.

"But why?" Aunt Jane questioned. "Why would you try to fool everyone?"

"I love my job," Ray said. "And I was afraid I'd lose it if the theater shut down."

"I don't understand." Aunt Jane shook her head in bewilderment. "What does that have to do with fooling everyone?"

Henry was ready with an answer. "It was a publicity stunt, wasn't it?"

"Yes, I thought it'd make headlines—and it did." Ray shrugged a little. "So there you have it. I'm guilty as charged."

"Honestly, Ray!" Fern rolled her eyes. "Alice wrote a brilliant play. Tickets would've sold without any help from you."

"And Fern's wowing the audience," put in Aunt Jane.

Ray couldn't argue. "You're right," he said. "We didn't need gimmicks to drum up ticket sales. I know that now."

"You did everything then?" asked Benny, who still couldn't get over it. "The popcorn, the hat hanging from the chandelier, the—"

"Not quite everything," Ray corrected. "I wasn't responsible for the missing tapes. That was all Tricia's doing."

Jessie nodded. "No wonder you looked so shocked when Benny found the tapes under his seat."

"I knew I hadn't put them there," Ray said, chuckling to himself. "It had me wondering if the theater really was haunted."

"I guess you got a taste of your own medicine." Fern gave him a sideways glance.

"Didn't you, Ray?"

"Yes, I guess I did." Ray turned to the actress. "Can you ever forgive me for what I've done, Fern?" he asked sheepishly.

Fern folded her arms in front of her and looked away without answering.

"Come on," Ray pleaded. "Don't be like that."

"For the life of me," Fern said, shaking her head, "I don't know why I should forgive you." Then a slow smile began to curl her lips. "But...all's well that ends well, I suppose," she said, softening a little.

Just then, there was a knock at the door. A muffled voice announced, "Two minutes, Miss Robson."

While Aunt Jane and the Aldens watched the rest of the play from the wings, Ray whispered, "I'm glad the truth is out about those pranks. It's a load off my mind."

"The truth is out about Alice Duncan too," added Aunt Jane. "Now everybody knows who really won the contest."

"Thanks to the Aldens!" said Ray.

When the curtain went down, Aunt Jane

turned to the director. "I think you have a real hit on your hands," she said, while a thunder of applause filled the theater.

As Fern took a bow, she gestured for the Aldens to join her on center stage.

"That's your cue, kids," Ray said, urging them on.

The four children came out from the wings just as Fern announced, "I give you...Henry, Jessie, Violet, and Benny!"

With the audience cheering, the Aldens took a bow.

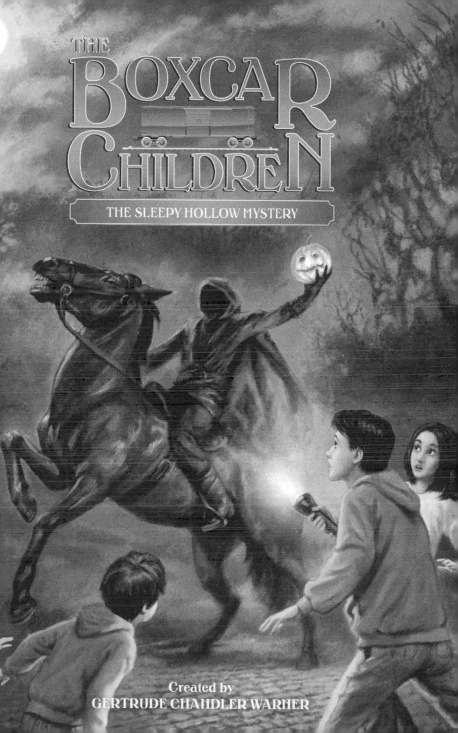

THE BOXCAR CHILDREN

THE SLEEPY HOLLOW MYSTERY

Created by
GERTRUDE CHANDLER WARNER

Contents

CHAPTER 1

Sleepy Hollow

The Haunted Hollow Gift Shop, located on the first floor of a big yellow house with white shutters, was completely dark when Mrs. McGregor parked the car in front of it.

"I thought Mrs. Vanderhoff was expecting us," Jessie Alden said, peering out the car window.

"She is," said Mrs. McGregor, the Alden's housekeeper. "I'm not surprised the shop is dark, since it's closed at night, but the lights in the upstairs apartment should be on."

Ten-year-old Violet Alden rolled down the car window and leaned out. "I think there's someone standing on the porch. It looks like a man in a cape, but he's standing very still."

Their dog, Watch, perched on Jessie's lap, began to growl.

The youngest Alden, Benny, asked, "Can I see?" He stuck his head out and then jerked back in, bumping against Violet. "Roll up the window, quick! The man doesn't have a head. It's there on the ground!"

His older brother, Henry, took a flashlight out of the glove compartment. "It's probably some sort of Halloween decoration." He shone the light on the front of the shop. "It's a scarecrow. He's headless, all right, but the thing on the ground is just a carved pumpkin."

Benny moved closer to Jessie. "The town of Sleepy Hollow is already turning out to be spooky."

"There *is* something strange about that pumpkin head," Violet said. "It's all white."

"Is it a ghost pumpkin?" Benny asked.

"I've seen white pumpkins at farm stands,"

Jessie told him. "Some people like them because they're unusual."

"I think I like the orange ones better," Benny declared. "No ghost pumpkins for me."

"Are we sure this the right day?" Violet asked. "Maybe Mrs. Vanderhoff thought we were coming a different day."

"No, I just talked to Gretchen on Tuesday. I told her your fall break started this Friday," Mrs. McGregor said. The Aldens' grandfather was away on a business trip, so Mrs. McGregor had brought them to the Hudson River Valley to visit one of her old friends, Mrs. Vanderhoff. The children were excited to see how the town of Sleepy Hollow celebrated Halloween, and they were looking forward to going on one of the new ghost tours run by Mrs. Vanderhoff's daughter.

Henry Alden snapped on Watch's leash and got out of the car with the dog. "Why don't we ring the doorbell?"

The rest of them followed.

"The apartment door is on the side of the building," Mrs. Vanderhoff said.

Before they could ring the bell, a figure carrying a lantern came out of the shadows between the buildings. Violet, who was in front, let out a little squeak of surprise and took a step back.

"Don't be frightened," a woman's voice called. As she came forward, the lantern light showed a woman about Mrs. McGregor's age.

"Gretchen!" Mrs. McGregor exclaimed. "We were worried when we didn't see any lights. Children, this is my dear friend Mrs. Vanderhoff."

Mrs. Vanderhoff said, "I'm delighted to meet you. Now let me guess who is who. I've heard so much about you."

"Guess me first! Please!" Benny raised his hand.

"Hmmm…well, I know Henry is fourteen years old. Are you Henry?" She smiled when she said this to Benny and the older children knew she was teasing.

"No." Benny laughed. "I'm only six."

"Then you must be Benny, and the taller boy must be Henry."

"You're right!" Benny said. "Can you guess

the girls?"

Mrs. Vanderhoff smiled again. "The girls are easier to guess because I've heard Violet likes purple and I see one of you has on a purple sweater."

Violet nodded.

"I also know you're an artist," Mrs. Vanderhoff continued. "I hope you brought your paints! The Hudson River Valley is a famous spot for painting."

"I did bring them," Violet said. "I would like to try to paint some of the trees with their fall colors."

Mrs. Vanderhoff turned to Violet's sister. "So you must be Jessie," she said, shaking Jessie's hand. "And I'd recognize Watch anywhere." She patted the dog, and the terrier wagged his tail. "I'm sorry it's so dark, but the power is out," she explained.

"The dark made your porch look scary," Benny said.

"We thought the scarecrow was a headless man," Violet added.

Mrs. Vanderhoff looked puzzled. "The scarecrow isn't supposed to be scary. My

daughter Annika carved a happy face on the pumpkin head."

"The pumpkin head is on the ground," Jessie said. Henry shone the flashlight so Mrs. Vanderhoff could see it.

"Oh, that's too bad. The pumpkin must have fallen off the scarecrow frame. Annika wouldn't make a headless scarecrow. She doesn't like scary Halloween decorations. We'll fix the scarecrow tomorrow. Now, if you want to bring your suitcases around back, I do have a nice fire going in the fire pit. I also have some hot cider for everyone. My other daughter Margot made some crullers today too. I think you will like those."

"I don't know what crullers are, but they sound good!" Benny said. "I'm hungry."

Mrs. Vanderhoff laughed. "Crullers are a special kind of doughnut dipped in sugar. The recipe has been in my family for generations, ever since the first Dutch settlers came to this area of New York."

"We can't wait to try them," Jessie said as she helped Henry get the suitcases out of the car.

Henry paused to look around. "The power isn't out anywhere else," he said. "That restaurant next door has all its lights on."

Mrs. Vanderhoff sighed. "The restaurant is the reason we don't have electricity. They are doing some repair work. Somehow the power to my property was cut off. It's supposed to be fixed in the morning, but until then, we'll have to rely on flashlights and candles."

A paved path led to a fenced-in backyard. Torches in the ground lit a stone patio with a fire pit in the center. The fire in it blazed away. Jessie thought it looked very cozy, like a little island of light in the dark yard.

"Take a seat," Mrs. Vanderhoff said, motioning to the benches placed around the fire. They all sat down except Watch, who stood next to Henry. The dog sniffed the air and then whined.

"Settle down, Watch," Henry said. He patted the dog, who sat down but continued to look around, his ears alert.

"Who would like hot cider?" Mrs. Vanderhoff asked.

"I would!" Benny said.

"I think we all would," Mrs. McGregor added.

Mrs. Vanderhoff went over to a small table that held a thermos, mugs, a large platter covered with foil, and a cookie jar. As she poured, she explained, "Annika will be back with her ghost-tour guests very soon. They walk most of the way, but then a friend of hers picks them up in an old wagon and brings them back here. When they arrive, everyone sits around the fire for snacks and one last story."

"How is the ghost-tour business going?" Mrs. McGregor asked.

Mrs. Vanderhoff handed a mug of cider to Benny. "Annika is just starting out so it's been a little slow. Her tours are unusual. She's calling them family-friendly ghost walks. So many young children think some parts of Halloween are too scary. She tells interesting stories and shows them some beautiful places in the woods."

"That's a good idea," Violet said. "Sometimes I'm scared of the dark. My friends like Halloween haunted houses, but I don't."

"Annika is hoping some of the people who take the tours will tell their friends," Mrs. Vanderhoff said. "Every little bit of money helps. My poor old house needs so many repairs. We fix one thing just when something else breaks."

"If you have some tools I can use," Henry said, "I'll be happy to fix what I can. I like to fix things."

"Thank you, Henry. I have several small jobs you could do. At least the apartment over the garage where you'll be staying is in good shape, except it doesn't have any power at the moment. If you are too frightened to stay out there, we can all stay inside the main house."

"We'll be fine," Jessie said. "We're used to staying in places without electricity. Our boxcar in the woods didn't have any power."

After their parents died, the Alden children had run away. They had never met their grandfather, but they were afraid of him because they'd heard he was mean. The children had found an abandoned boxcar in the woods and made it their home. When their grandfather found them, they realized he wasn't mean at all. He brought them to his home to live with him and Mrs. McGregor. He even had the boxcar moved to his backyard.

Mrs. Vanderhoff's cell phone rang. She answered and a serious look appeared on her face. "Oh dear. Margot isn't home, but I'll be there right away." Putting the phone away, she said, "That was Annika. Her friend Isiah didn't show up with the wagon and she can't reach him. I need to go pick up the tour group and bring them back here."

"Will everyone fit in your car?" Mrs. McGregor asked. "I can take my car too."

"Thank you. I was going to have to take two trips," Mrs. Vanderhoff said. "You children will be fine here by yourselves for a little while, won't you?"

"I guess so. You'll be back soon, right?" Benny asked. "It is very dark even with the fire."

Jessie put her arm around him. "We'll be fine," she assured him. But she looked around at the trees with their twisted branches looming over the yard and hoped they wouldn't have to stay alone for *too* long.

"Have a cruller or a cookie while you're waiting." Mrs. Vanderhoff motioned to the covered platter and the cookie jar. "There are plenty."

After Mrs. Vanderhoff and Mrs. McGregor left, Jessie finished pouring the cider for everyone and asked, "Which do you want, cookies or crullers?" She tried to sound cheerful so the others wouldn't realize she was already getting a little spooked about being in such a dark, strange place.

"I think we should try something new, so I vote for the crullers," Henry said.

Jessie passed them out. "I like the shape of these. They look like someone braided pieces of dough."

"These are yummy," Violet said, biting into hers. "They're so much crunchier that regular doughnuts."

"I like the sugar that's all over them!" Benny said.

"Maybe I can get the recipe from Mrs.

Vanderhoff," Jessie said. "I can try to make them."

The wind picked up and the branches of the trees rustled. Most of them had already lost their leaves, but a few fell from a big oak tree and blew onto the patio. Watch leaped up and tried to catch some.

"I'm glad we have a fire." Jessie shivered, buttoning the top button of her coat. "It's chilly." The moving branches of the trees threw shadows on the ground, and they looked like broken skeletons dancing in the circle of light from the fire.

Just then Violet jumped, spilling some of her drink on the ground.

Henry was so startled, he almost dropped his drink too. "Violet! What's wrong?"

"Did you hear that noise?"

Chapter 2

A Headless Horseman

Henry said, "I don't hear anything but the wind." He listened and for a moment thought he heard a low rumble of thunder coming from down the street. It stopped, and he decided his ears must have been playing tricks on him.

"I don't hear anything either," Jessie said.

Violet was quiet for a moment and then asked, "You didn't hear anything that sounded sort of like an animal snorting, did you?"

Benny made pig noises and then asked,

"You mean like that?" Henry and Jessie laughed.

"No, not like that," Violet said. "It's hard to explain. Listen again."

They all sat quietly again, but there were no noises except the wind and the leaves blowing across the patio. Watch had stopped chasing them. He sat next to Henry with his ears alert.

"I still don't hear anything," Jessie said.

"Me neither." Benny took another bite of his cruller.

"I guess I imagined it." Violet scooted her bench closer to the fire.

Watch got up and walked toward the edge of the patio. He pulled on the end of the leash in Henry's hands.

"I think you can let go of his leash," Jessie said. "He can't get outside the fence." As soon as Henry let go, Watch slunk down on his belly. He crept over to the side of the yard growling softly.

"That's the direction I heard the noise," Violet whispered.

"Watch, what do you see?" Henry got up

and walked over to the fence. He shined the flashlight into the area behind the café next door. "I don't see anything. Silly Watch. It's just the wind." He listened for the thunder sound, and for an instant he thought he heard it again. It stopped, so he came back and sat down. They all huddled around the fire, which no longer seemed as bright.

Soon after, they heard the sound of cars, and then voices as a group of people came into the back yard.

Jessie was relieved to hear Mrs. Vanderhoff's voice. "The tour group is back!" Jessie told the others.

A young woman wearing a red velvet cape and carrying a lantern led the group to the patio. "Welcome to our house," she said. Even though she was smiling, her voice was a little shaky. Her wavy blond hair was falling out of the bun on top of her head.

She smiled at the Aldens, said hello, and told her group, "These are friends of the family. Why don't you all sit down and I'll serve you some treats." There were two sets of parents and three children in the group, but none of them looked like they were having fun.

The oldest child was girl about Benny's age and she was wearing a pretty princess costume, but Violet thought the girl was the most unhappy-looking princess she had ever seen. A little boy about two or three years old was dressed as a dragon. As the group walked to the patio, the boy grabbed hold of his father's leg and hid his face.

"We can help," Violet said, jumping up. Mrs. Vanderhoff handed her the cookie jar. Violet pulled the lid off and offered the jar to the third child, a little girl dressed like a mouse, who had sat down in the spot next to Violet's.

The girl reached her hand in and then jerked it back out. She screamed, "Gross! It's full of something yucky. I think there are worms and dirt in there."

Violet peered into the cookie jar. "It does have something in it besides cookies," she said. She sniffed it. "It doesn't smell like dirt though."

Jessie came over. "Can I look?" Violet

held it out to her and Jessie looked inside. "It smells like chocolate and some sort of fruit smell." She reached her hand in and pulled out something sticky. "This isn't really a worm. It's gummy candy meant to look like a worm. And I think the dirt is just crushed up chocolate cookies. We had treats like this at school last year for Halloween."

She looked at Mrs. Vanderhoff, who looked at Annika.

Annika said, "I don't know how those got in there. I filled the jar up with cookies myself."

"I guess it's a joke," Henry said.

"It's not a funny joke," the little girl's mother said as she took her daughter's hand. "This ghost tour is not turning out the way we expected."

"I'm sorry," Annika said. "I don't know who would play a trick like that."

A shriek rang out from the alley. It sounded like an angry scream.

Everyone stood up. A horse neighed, and they could hear hooves pounding. Watch began to bark. The boy dressed as a dragon cried out and his father picked him up. The Aldens and Annika ran to the fence at the back of the yard. The rest of the group but the scared toddler and his father followed them. They saw a big black horse come rushing down the alley. The horse's rider wore a black cape that billowed out in the wind.

"There's something not right about the rider," Violet said.

Henry shone the flashlight at the person on the horse.

"The rider doesn't have a head!" Benny cried. They all jumped back in surprise.

As the horse passed by the fence, the rider took something from inside the cape and held it up.

It resembled a head with glowing teeth and eyes. The rider heaved the head toward the group.

They all dodged away, bumping into one another. It landed with a thud in front of them. It split open, spraying them all with thick red liquid.

All three of the children from the tour group begin to sob.

"Don't cry," Jessie said. "It was just a pumpkin.."

One of the mothers held out her hands, which were speckled with red. "It looks like blood!"

Violet held out one of the pieces of the pumpkin. It was coated on the inside with

the red liquid. "That's not blood. It's paint. I can smell it." She turned it over. "And look at this on the outside that looks like an eye. It's glow-in-the-dark paint."

The woman said to Annika, "Young lady, that was a terrible trick. You advertise this as a ghost tour for families, but look at all the children crying. This was far too frightening. They'll have nightmares tonight."

"I'm so sorry," Annika said. "That horseman was not part of the tour. I don't know who it was, or why he would do something like that."

The woman took hold of her children's hands. "I don't believe some headless horseman from a story just happened to show up to throw a pumpkin at us. I will not be recommending this tour to any of our friends. In fact, I'm going to post a review online. People should know this is not for families. Let's go, everyone."

After the group left, Annika looked like she was going to cry. Mrs. Vanderhoff put her arm around her daughter's shoulders. "I'm sorry about the awful trick."

Henry picked up another piece of the pumpkin. "This is another one of those strange pumpkins. It's white, just like the ones in front."

"I use white pumpkins for the logo of my ghost-tour business," Annika said. "Whoever played this trick must have used a white pumpkin on purpose. They aren't easy to find."

"I wonder if the same person put the cookie crumbs and worm candy in the cookie jar," Jessie said.

"Who would have been able to do that?" Henry asked.

"I don't know," Annika brushed her hair off her face. More of it had fallen out of the bun. "We always have treats out here after the tours. I set everything up early so I don't have to rush around when we get back. I don't know who would have come into the backyard."

"Sometimes people play tricks around Halloween," Violet said. "Maybe that's all it is."

"I don't know," Henry said. "This kind of

trick would take a lot of effort. It's a really mean, scary trick. Why would anyone do that to Annika?"

A ghostly voice came from the path. "I'm coming to haunt you!"

Benny grabbed Jessie's hand. "Who...who said that?"

CHAPTER 3

The First Clue

"Isiah, stop with the voices," Annika called. She sounded angry.

A very tall and skinny young man came around the side of the house. He wore a black suit with a ruffled shirt and a tall black hat.

When he saw the Aldens and Mrs. McGregor, he swept his hat off his head and bowed. "Isiah Sanders at your service."

Violet whispered to Benny. "He looks like a character from a book."

"Where have you been?" Annika asked.

"You were supposed to drive the wagon!"

"You're mad at me, aren't you?" Isiah dropped down to his knees in front of her and clasped his hands in front of him. "Please forgive me," he begged. "I can't go on unless you do." He looked over at the Aldens and winked.

The children laughed at the performance.

"Oh, get up, Isiah," Annika said. "Now is not the time for acting."

He did, brushing the dirt off his knees. "I'm sorry I missed the tour. The harness on the wagon broke, and I lost my phone. I was coming to meet you with my car when the tire went flat. Why is it so dark? And where is the tour group?"

Henry thought Annika's friend was making a lot of excuses. It was hard to believe that so many bad things could happen to one person in such a short time.

Annika explained, "We heard some spooky noises in the woods on the first part of the tour. It sounded like there was something or someone out there following us. The tour guests weren't happy at all. And then you weren't there with the wagon."

"Are you sure the sounds you heard in the woods weren't just from an animal?" Henry asked.

"It sounded like a very big animal, even bigger than a deer," Annika said. "And deer don't make that much noise."

"That's a mean trick for someone to play," Isiah said.

"It was. I wish you had been there. You have to be more careful with your phone," Annika scolded. "I need someone I can count on to help me with the tours."

"Let me make it up to you. I'll lead the next tour and you take the easy job and drive the wagon. You know I'm good at telling stories and doing voices." He hunched over and then spoke in creaky, trembly voice like an old man. "I'll have them quivering in their boots." He pointed at Benny with a crooked finger. "Young man, you there? I see a strange, ghostly shape. Right behind you!" he yelled. Benny jumped, twisting around to look.

Benny's eyes opened wide and then he smiled. "I knew there wasn't really anyone there. I'm not that easy to trick."

"Just teasing you, young lad." Isiah laughed. "See, I'm good, aren't I?"

Annika stomped her foot and scowled at him. "This is supposed to be a family-friendly ghost tour, Isiah. Remember? We don't want them quivering in their boots."

"The tour has to be a little bit scary or else no one will want to go," Isiah said. "Can I have a cookie?" He reached for the cookie jar and then stopped. Jessie noticed a funny expression cross Isiah's face. "Come to think of it," Isiah said. "I'd rather have a cruller. I'm hungry."

Annika sighed. "You're the only person I know who is always hungry."

"You know two people now!" Benny said. "I'm always hungry too."

"There, you see," Isiah said, holding up his hand to high-five Benny. "Some people just need to eat. I should be going. I promise I'll be there tomorrow." He said good-bye to everyone.

After he left, Annika slumped down on one of the benches. "I guess the ghost-tour business was a bad idea. Maybe I should just quit."

"No, it's too soon to give up," Mrs. Vanderhoff told her.

"Can we go with you tomorrow?" Henry asked. "We might be able to help find out who is playing tricks."

"That's a good idea," Mrs. McGregor said. "If anyone can help solve this mystery, it's these four."

"You can come," Annika said. "But I don't think it will help."

"Annika, you sound very tired." Mrs. Vanderhoff said. "Things will seem better in the morning." She got up. "Why don't we all go to bed?"

She took the Aldens up to the apartment and showed them the sleeping bags on the floor. "I set everything up for you before it got dark. There are flashlights for each of you on the table and extra blankets on the sofa. Are you sure you'll be all right?"

"We'll be fine," Jessie said.

"Good night, then." After she left, Watch inspected each sleeping bag. He picked a dark green one and then lay down on it, closing his eyes.

"Watch is tired too," Violet said. "Someone is going to have to share their bed with him."

"I will," Benny said. "He can watch out for me. Watch can watch me, get it?"

"That's good, Benny," Violet said. "Let's all go to bed. I'm as tired as Watch."

Once they were all in their pajamas, Benny asked, "That wasn't really a headless horseman, was it?"

"No, it was someone dressed up like that," Jessie said. "There's an old story about a headless horseman by an author named Washington Irving. It's set in Sleepy Hollow. We read it in school."

"I don't know why someone would want to dress up like that," Benny grumbled. "It's too scary."

"We'll find out who did it and then you'll see it's just a trick," Henry said.

***

They woke the next morning when Mrs. McGregor came in the door. She had a tray with mugs of hot chocolate. "Good morning! The power is still out, but as soon as you're dressed, we're going next door to the restaurant for breakfast. I hear they have very tasty apple pancakes."

Benny jumped up. "Let's go!"

"Not in pajamas!" Jessie said, laughing.

"Oh, right," Benny said, looking down at his pajamas. "I forgot."

Mrs. McGregor picked up Watch's leash. "I'll take Watch and give him his breakfast," she said. "He can stay in the backyard while we go to the café. Come along, Watch."

When the Aldens were ready, they walked over to the café with Mrs. Vanderhoff and Mrs. McGregor. "Annika won't be joining us," Mrs. Vanderhoff said. "I'm afraid she has a bad headache. She is still upset about last night."

"I'd be upset too," Jessie said.

"Yes, we don't like when people play mean tricks," Henry added.

In front of the café a man wearing a jacket and a tie was watching two workers attaching a sign to a post outside the restaurant. The sign had a big red apple on it.

"I can read the sign!" Benny said. "It's called the Apple House Café!"

"Good job, Benny," Jessie said. "You're learning fast."

"Good morning, Mr. Beekman," Mrs. Vanderhoff said. "What a nice new sign."

The man mumbled something and then turned away from them.

Mrs. Vanderhoff shook her head sadly at the man's reaction and said, "Let's go on in."

As they walked up the steps, one of the workmen said, "This paint isn't dry! It's all over my hands. We shouldn't be putting up this sign now."

"I want it done today," Mr. Beekman said. "Put it up and I'll repaint it if it needs it."

He added something else, but the Aldens couldn't hear because a hostess opened the door of the café and said, "Welcome to the Apple House Café." She showed them to a big round table in the back and gave them menus.

A few minutes later a waiter in a red apron appeared. He scowled at them. Violet thought he looked a little like the man outside, but much younger. Both had curly brown hair and round faces.

"Good morning, Brett," Mrs. Vanderhoff said.

The young man didn't respond to her greeting as he pulled out an order pad. "We're busy," he snapped. "There's going to be a long wait for your food. What do you want?" He took down their orders for pancakes, eggs, bacon, coffee, and orange juice before hurrying away.

"The people who work here don't seem very friendly," Violet said.

"It's just Brett and his father," Mrs. Vanderhoff said. "I'm afraid they aren't very happy with me. They offered to buy my house at a good price. They want to turn it into a bed and breakfast for Brett to run. I just don't want to sell. I love my little shop, even if it doesn't make much money."

"Could Mr. Beekman be the one playing the tricks?" Henry asked. "He may think the tricks will convince you to sell the house."

"We know he has red paint," Violet said.

"And someone who owns a restaurant might know about food that looks like worms and dirt," Jessie added.

"Oh, I hope he wouldn't do that." Mrs. Vanderhoff looked shocked. "That wouldn't be very neighborly. I'm sure it's someone else."

Brett stomped over with a coffee pot and a pitcher of juice. He set the juice down with a thunk and some of it sloshed onto the tablecloth. "Oops," he said as he walked away.

The Aldens looked at each other. They weren't so sure.

CHAPTER 4

The Lost Scarecrow

A young woman came into the café and waved when she saw them.

"That's my other daughter Margot," Mrs. Vanderhoff said.

"She looks like Annika," Mrs. McGregor said. Margot had wavy blond hair like Annika but she looked a few years older.

When Margot sat down, Mrs. Vanderhoff introduced everyone and added, "Margot can tell you about Sleepy Hollow. She works for the county tourist office. She knows all about the history of the place and the wonderful things to see in the area."

"You've come to visit us at the right time," Margot said. "Halloween is the spookiest time of year in the spookiest town in America."

"Is Sleepy Hollow really the spookiest town?" Benny asked.

"It will be if I have my way," Margot said. "There's a contest going on in a travel magazine. I'm submitting an entry for our town. If we win, more tourists will visit us."

"How will the contest be judged?" Jessie asked. "Isn't it hard to prove a place is spooky?"

"I'll send in some of the pictures I've been taking of scary places and scary things around town. I'm also writing down all the unexplained hauntings we've had. The headless horseman from last night is a perfect story."

"Your sister was very upset by that," Mrs. Vanderhoff said.

"She shouldn't have been." Margot looked annoyed. "I don't think her ghost-tour business is going to work. It's silly to have a ghost tour that's not scary."

"You should support your sister's idea,"

Mrs. Vanderhoff said. "Annika is trying very hard to earn some money for the house repairs. We need a new roof."

"Mother, you should just sell the house to Mr. Beekman," Margot said. "You could use the money to rent a shop in a better location right downtown, and get yourself an apartment. Then you wouldn't have to worry about the roof. Plus, the town needs a gift shop on the main street."

"I love our house. It's been in our family too long to sell it because it requires some work." She poured herself some coffee. "Would you please pass me the sugar, Violet?"

Violet handed the bowl and its tongs to Mrs. Vanderhoff. Benny watched with interest as Mrs. Vanderhoff used the tongs to take a sugar cube out of the sugar bowl. She dropped it into her coffee.

"I didn't know sugar came in little blocks like that," Benny said. "Can I try one?"

"Just one," Jessie said. "Too much sugar isn't good for you."

He popped on in his mouth. "This is a good treat!"

Just then Brett brought their breakfasts. "Pancakes will be a better treat," Jessie said. She handed the syrup to Benny.

He poured the syrup on his pancakes and then took a big bite of one. "Even if the people aren't nice here, they make good pancakes."

Mrs. Vanderhoff smiled. "I'm glad you like them. Maybe after breakfast you children would like to make a scarecrow. There's a scarecrow contest at the library this afternoon. Annika made one, and we have all the supplies to build another."

"That would be so much fun!" Violet said.

"I'll be there taking pictures," Margot said. "There are always some amazing scarecrows in the contest."

Mrs. Vanderhoff turned to Henry. "We have wood for you to make a frame for the scarecrow. While you're doing that, your brother and sisters can look in the attic for old clothes to dress it up."

"Do we have to make a scary scarecrow?" Benny asked. "I'm not sure I want to do that."

"No, you can make any kind of scarecrow you like," Mrs. Vanderhoff said.

When they were finished with breakfast, she took them over to the house and up to the attic. "Use anything you want. The old trunks are full of clothes. If you need anything, just come downstairs and ask."

"I'll go make the frame," Henry said. "When you find something to put on the scarecrow you can bring it out to the garage. We can stuff it full of straw out there."

Jessie opened one of the trunks. "Should we make a girl scarecrow? There are some good dresses here."

"How about a lady in purple?" Violet suggested, picking up a long purple dress.

"Okay," Benny agreed. "That's not scary."

"Here's a good hat for her." Jessie said. She pulled out a big straw hat with a pink bow on it.

The three of them went to find Henry. He had already finished the frame and was putting away the tools while Watch followed him around. The children took the frame out into the yard, dressed the scarecrow, and stuffed it with straw.

When they were finished, Watch came over and growled at it.

"Watch doesn't like scarecrows," Violet said.

"It's because it doesn't have a head," Benny said. "I don't like headless scarecrows either. How do we fix it?"

"We could stuff a paper bag to use as the head," Jessie suggested. She went inside to ask Mrs. Vanderhoff for one and returned with a large grocery bag.

"Now it needs a face," Henry said.

Violet said, "I'll get my art supplies." She

brought down her markers and drew a lady's face onto the paper bag. When she was done, Henry attached the head to the scarecrow. Jessie put the hat on it. They stood back to look.

"It doesn't look quite right," Henry said. "But I don't know why."

Jessie laughed. "We forgot something important! It's missing hair!"

"How can we make hair?" Benny asked. "Bald scarecrows are almost as scary as headless ones."

"Maybe Mrs. Vanderhoff has some yarn," Violet suggested.

Mrs. Vanderhoff had yarn in shades of green, pink, and orange. "Let's use pink," Violet said. "That goes with the bow on the hat."

When they were done, they carried it around to the front of the house and onto the porch. Mrs. Vanderhoff and Mrs. McGregor came outside.

"What a wonderful scarecrow!" Mrs. Vanderhoff exclaimed. "It will stand out in the crowd."

The Aldens spent the rest of the morning helping Mrs. Vanderhoff in the shop. Jessie dusted while Benny and Violet made black and orange paper chains to decorate the front windows. Henry fixed a loose hinge on the door to the storeroom. Annika came downstairs when she felt better and helped too.

After lunch, Henry and Jessie loaded the scarecrow into Annika's car. She drove them downtown to the library. The lawn in front was filled with rows and rows of colorful scarecrows.

"Look at that one with the big red nose!" Benny said. "It's a clown scarecrow. I see one that looks like a cowboy. I'm glad there are scarecrows that aren't scary."

"Is there room for ours?" Violet asked.

"We'll ask Isiah," Annika said. "He works at the library and is organizing the contest this year."

"Is that him?" Benny pointed at a man wearing a wizard costume with a long white beard.

"Yes, he loves any excuse to dress up,"

Annika said. "He wants to be a professional actor some day."

Isiah saw them coming and hurried over to meet them. "What a great scarecrow," he said. "Or maybe we should call it a scare lady. Would you like to dance, miss?" He took the scarecrow from Henry and twirled it around.

Everyone laughed.

When he stopped, Jessie asked, "Where can we put it?"

Isiah handed the scarecrow back to Henry. "I've put plenty of poles, so let's find one that isn't claimed yet."

They found a spot in one of the back rows and set up the scarecrow. When they were finished, they went to look at the other contestants.

"There's Margot taking pictures," Jessie pointed.

Margot looked up and waved at them.

Loud voices made them turn toward the street. A group of young men piled out of a car, laughing and joking with one another. "There's Brett Beekman from the restaurant," Violet said, motioning to one of them.

The four young men ambled up to the scarecrows. One of them laughed and pointed at a scarecrow in an old ripped dress. "That looks like the old lady who works in the library," he said.

"It looks better than the old lady," another one said.

They all laughed and then Brett yelled, "There's Margot! Margot, take a picture of us! We're more interesting than scarecrows."

She rolled her eyes and ignored them.

"They're rude, aren't they?" Benny said to Violet. Violet nodded her head.

Brett and his friends drew closer. Brett pulled a witch scarecrow off its stake. "Who's scared of witches? She's going to get you." He swung it close to Violet and Benny and said, "Better run, kiddies, before the witch turns you into a couple of toads." Jerking it toward them, he yelled, "Boo!"

Benny jumped and cried out, "Stop!"

Brett's friends laughed again. Jessie crossed her arms in front of her and frowned. "Stop that. You're scaring my little brother."

"I'm just teasing," Brett said.

"It's mean teasing," Henry said.

Isiah rushed over to them. "Put that scarecrow back!" he ordered Brett. When Brett didn't move, Isiah grabbed it from his hands. "What are you doing here? This doesn't seem like your kind of fun."

"We can go wherever we want." Brett stared at Isiah's costume. "Why don't you dress in normal clothes? You look like a freak."

Isiah looked angry. "I've got a job to do, a real job, not one my father got for me."

Brett clenched his fists and took a step toward Isiah.

"Stop, you two," Annika said. "Brett, why don't you leave Isiah alone? You've been mean to him for years. Don't you get tired of it?"

"I'm just joking around," Brett said. "He's the one who can't take a joke." He walked away to join his friends.

"Let's forget about him," Jessie said. "Annika, where is your scarecrow?"

"I don't know where Isiah put it," Annika said. "But it should be easy to find. It looks just like the one in front of the shop."

"It's in the second row on the end," Isiah said. He put the witch scarecrow back on the pole. "I'll show you."

They followed after him to the end of the row, but the pole was empty. There was no headless scarecrow in a black cape. "That's strange," Isiah said. "I know it was here yesterday afternoon."

"Maybe someone moved it," Benny said.

"We'll look for it," said Jessie.

"Let's split up," Henry suggested.

A few minutes later, Jessie motioned for the rest to join her. "I found it," she said. "It's under a pine tree on the side of the library."

"Why would anyone move it there?" Annika asked.

Jessie didn't answer the question. "You should come look," she said in a low voice, her eyes darting around the crowd, "but I don't think we should let anyone else see it. It's bad."

CHAPTER 5

Beware

Henry, Violet, and Benny followed Jessie.

As they drew closer, Violet asked, "Why is the straw scattered everywhere?"

"Someone took out all the straw!" Benny said.

"That's not the worst." Jessie pointed at the pumpkin head. It had been smashed, and spattered with the same fake blood. It lay in pieces scattered around the scarecrow's body.

"What's that?" Benny asked, pointing a

trembling finger at a piece of paper on the scarecrow's chest.

Henry knelt down. "It's a note." He pulled it free and held it up. The word *BEWARE* was scrawled on it in the same color as the spattered red.

"That's horrible," Violet shuddered.

"Even if it's just a scarecrow, it's a bad thing to do," Benny said.

"What's going on back here?" Margot's voice came from behind them.

"Someone ruined my scarecrow," Annika told her sister.

Margot smiled when she saw the scarecrow on the ground. "Wow! What a great picture this will make." She snapped several pictures.

"Margot! Is that all you can think of?" Annika cried. "Someone did this on purpose."

"I can use it in the 'Most Haunted Town in America' entry. Can you children move out of the way so I can get a better shot?" Margot took more photos, which attracted the attention of the people admiring the scarecrows in the contest. Soon, a crowd of people was gathered around the damaged scarecrow.

"Annika, isn't that your ghost-tour scarecrow?" a woman asked.

Annika nodded. "Yes. I don't know who would do this."

"Why does it say *BEWARE*?" a boy asked. "Does it mean beware of the ghost tour?"

"No," Annika said. "I think it's just someone playing a joke. My ghost tours are fun and not scary."

"That's not what I've heard," the woman said. "I heard the last one frightened several children." Annika tried to explain but the woman wouldn't listen. "We won't be going on it," she said as she walked away.

The Aldens helped Annika pick up the pieces of her scarecrow. They could tell she was discouraged.

"Don't worry, Annika," Jessie said. "We're determined to find out who is playing these tricks."

"Who could have had a chance to move the scarecrow?" Henry asked.

"Anyone," Annika's face was glum. "I helped Isiah put it up yesterday. Someone could have moved it in the night. Let's go home."

Back at the house, the Aldens raked leaves for Mrs. Vanderhoff. When they were finished, Jessie got a notebook out of her suitcase. "Let's write down what we know about these terrible tricks and who could have done them," she said.

"Even though Mrs. Vanderhoff thinks Mr. Beekman wouldn't play the tricks, we should add him to the list," Henry said.

"And Brett too," Violet added. "He is very rude and mean."

"We should add the headless horseman to the list," Benny said.

"Benny, you know there's no real headless horseman," Jessie told him. "It's just a story."

"We've seen a headless horseman," Benny insisted. "He needs to be on the list."

"All right, I'll add him, but we need to think of other possibilities." Jessie wrote *headless horseman* in her notebook.

"What about Margot?" Henry asked. "She wants to get the town named the spookiest in America. She knows all about how Annika does the tours. She could have put the cookie crumbs and the candy worms in the cookie jar."

"But Margot is Annika's sister!" Violet shook her head. "That would be too mean."

"Maybe Margot doesn't realize it is mean," Henry said. "She might think it will help Annika's business if the town is named the spookiest."

"When Margot saw Annika's scarecrow, she didn't seem to notice that Annika was upset," Jessie added. "Mrs. Vanderhoff said Margot should have been at home last night when Annika called. Since she wasn't there, *she* could have ridden the horse. I'll write her name down too."

Mrs. Vanderhoff called them for dinner before they could think of more names. They ate quickly so they would be ready for the ghost tour. After dinner, Mrs. McGregor said, "I'll feed Watch and put him up in the apartment until you get back. Mrs. Vanderhoff and I are going to visit some of her friends, so we might not be back until after you are home."

"Poor Watch. I'm sorry you have to stay home," Benny said.

"Don't worry about Watch," Mrs. McGregor said. "He's been chasing squirrels all afternoon in the backyard. I'm sure he's very tired."

When everyone had their coats on, they walked with Annika to the tour's meeting point. A group of eight people arrived for the tour, four adults and four children, two girls and two boys. The boys were twins. One of the little girls announced, "I'm the birthday girl. I'm five."

"I'm five too," the twins said together.

The other girl said, "I'm almost five. I think." She looked up at her mother.

"Almost," her mother said. "In a year." Everyone laughed.

Annika wore her cape and carried a lantern with a candle in it. "I have a box of battery powered lanterns too," she said. "Anyone who might feel scared can carry one of these. I want you to have fun." All the younger children asked for lanterns, including Benny and Violet.

As they walked into the woods, Annika told them stories from the town's history. "People used to think there was a witch who lived in the forest," she said. "But she turned out to be something very different." Before she could finish the story, a loud cracking noise came from the trees on the side of the path. The group stopped.

"I think I saw something in the trees," one of the twins said. "Something big."

"Sometimes it's easy to imagine you see something when it's just the trees," Jessie told him. "It could be just a clump of bushes."

"Jessie is right," Annika said. "Let's keep going." She smiled, but the Aldens knew she was worried. They walked on, though everyone seemed a little nervous. Annika started her story again when another cracking noise came from behind them.

A sudden shriek startled them all. Everyone spun around, trying to see what had made the awful noise.

"That might have been an animal," Henry said.

Far down the path, a large, dark shape burst out of the woods. It made a loud snorting sound.

Everyone all stood very still.

Two red circles of light appeared, glowing in the dark.

"Are those eyes?" Violet whispered.

"I think so," Benny said. "But what has red eyes?"

"If those are eyes, that thing would have to be about ten feet tall," Henry said.

The lights disappeared, but the shape moved toward them. It came slowly at first and then faster and faster. It shrieked again.

"We should get off the path," Jessie yelled.

They all rushed into the woods just as the creature thundered past them. They could see it was a horse with a rider who wore a cape. In the light of Annika's lantern, they could see that the rider didn't seem to have a head.

The youngest girl in the group screamed and ran to her mother. One of the twins burst into tears. The parents of the twins each rushed to pick up one of the little boys.

"Pick me up too, Daddy!" the older girl said as she held up her arms to him.

"Please calm down," Annika said. "I'm sorry, but that was someone playing a trick." She sounded like she was going to cry too.

"We know that was just a horse," Henry

said, stepping back out onto the path. "Horses don't have glowing red eyes. We should see if we can find any clues about who is playing these tricks." He started to jog toward where the horse and its rider had first appeared on the path.

"Henry, I can't let you do that," Annika called after him.

"I'll just be a minute," Henry replied over his shoulder

"No!" Annika yelled. She ran after him and grabbed his sleeve when she caught up. "I'm responsible for you. Let's just stay calm and meet Isiah. The wagon will be waiting for us."

Henry could tell she was very upset. "All right, but I'm sure there is nothing dangerous back there."

Violet turned and looked in the other direction. "I hope Isiah is okay," she said. "The horse and rider will be riding right past where he's waiting with the wagon."

Annika tried to smile at the parents and children. "I'm…I'm sure he's fine. Jessie, would you and Benny walk with the group while Violet and Henry and I go ahead to make sure Isiah is...is ready for us?"

Jessie nodded. She was frightened but she knew Annika wanted her to be brave.

Henry and Violet followed Annika down the path, scared at what they might find. When they came to the wagon, they didn't see Isiah.

"What if the headless rider got him?" Violet asked.

Annika called out, "Isiah, where are you?"

CHAPTER 6

Costumes and More Clues

"I'm right here," Isiah called, sounding out of breath. He came around from the front of the wagon. "I was adjusting Ghost's harness."

"Did you see the horse run by?" Henry asked.

"What horse?" Isiah looked very puzzled.

"A big black horse chased us off the path!" Violet said. "It would have dashed right past you. It was making a horrible noise too."

"I didn't see anything," Isiah said. "I didn't hear anything either. I always listen to music while I'm waiting." He patted his coat pocket. "I keep my MP3 player and my earbuds with me. Though the horses were both restless for some reason."

Henry thought Isiah sounded like he was telling the truth, but Henry couldn't figure out what had happened to the horse. He supposed it might have gone off the path into the woods, just like it had appeared onto the path.

Jessie, Benny, and the rest of the group arrived. The children were no longer crying, but none of them were smiling.

Isiah bowed to the tour group and said, "Good evening. Ghost and Spook and I welcome you." He motioned to the two white horses hitched to a big open wagon. No one said anything. He held his lantern up and looked around at the group. "Looks like we have a quiet crowd tonight. No one is laughing. Shall I tell you a funny story?"

"No," Annika said. "We should just go back to the shop." She helped the smaller children into the wagon.

"Isiah, did you fall down?" Benny asked.

"You have mud on your face and your coat is ripped."

Annika turned and examined Isiah. "Benny is right. What happened?"

Isiah rubbed his muddy cheek. "Benny guessed it. I'm just clumsy. When I got out of the wagon to tighten the harness, I slipped in the mud."

Jessie started to speak and then stopped. It hadn't rained since they had been in Sleepy Hollow, and she didn't see any mud. She would note it in her notebook when she got back to the Vanderhoffs.

On the way back, Annika tried to teach the tour group an old folk song. The Aldens joined in but the other children were still fearful. They held up their lanterns and looked out into the darkness. Jessie could hear the parents grumbling to each other about the scare they'd had. When the tour arrived back to the house, the group didn't want to stay for the treats and asked for their money back. Annika gave it to them, apologizing.

When the tour group was gone, Isiah

said, "Now are you going to tell me what happened?"

Annika started to cry, so Henry explained what had happened.

"Not another trick," Isiah groaned.

"We were worried the horseman would get you," Violet said.

"Annika, you should really let me do the tours," Isiah said. "Look how upset you are."

"No, I can do them." Annika wiped her face. "I'm not going to let someone scare me with silly tricks."

"All right, but think about it." Isiah patted his horses. "I should get these old boys back to the stable. It's getting late."

After Isiah left, the Aldens helped Annika put away the treats and drinks. They were nearly finished when Violet said, "I hear a noise. I think someone is in the yard behind Mr. Beekman's café."

Henry walked to the fence. "Hello!" he called out, shining the flashlight.

"What do you want?" a man said in an angry voice. "Don't shine that light in my eyes."

"It's Mr. Beekman," Annika said. She

went over to the fence. "Good evening, Mr. Beekman. We were just worried when we heard a noise."

"Well, I'm allowed to go into my café whenever I want. I came to get something I'd forgotten."

"Sorry we bothered you," Henry said.

When they had finished cleaning up, Annika said, "Thank you for helping. I'm very tired, and I need to think about what to do about the tours. Good night."

The Aldens went up to the apartment. Henry looked out the window. "Mr. Beekman is leaving. He said he came to get something, but he's not carrying anything."

"Maybe it's something small, like a piece of paper he put in his pocket," Violet suggested.

"We have to figure this out," Henry said. "Annika was very upset tonight. If it happens again, she might stop her ghost tours."

Jessie told them about the lack of mud around the wagon. "I'm adding Isiah to the list," she said.

"We do know he likes to dress up in costumes," Violet said thoughtfully. "He likes to act too. Whoever is playing the tricks is good at pretending to be the headless horseman."

"Why would he play a trick on Annika?" Benny asked. "They are supposed to be friends. I like Isiah."

"I do too." Jessie took her notebook out but didn't write anything down.

"He really wants to be the one who does the ghost tours." Henry said, turning away from the window. "Maybe he's hoping she'll be so scared that she'll let him lead the tours."

"If Isiah had been riding a black horse, where did he put it?" Jessie asked. "We know it wasn't Ghost or Spook. You can't make white horses look black."

"That's part of the mystery," Violet said.

Jessie wrote down Isiah's name, but the rest of the Aldens could tell she didn't like his name on the list.

***

The next morning Jessie and the other children helped Mrs. Vanderhoff make more crullers.

"There are many different kinds of crullers, but I think my family's recipe is the best," Mrs. Vanderhoff said as they mixed the flour and cinnamon and other ingredients. "The shape is important. First, you take a piece of dough and roll it between your hands until it looks like piece of rope." She gave each of the Aldens their own dough to work with. Jessie did hers and then helped Benny.

When everyone had the dough in the right shape, Mrs. Vanderhoff showed them how to fold each piece in two so the dough looked like a braid. "Next we cut them into sections and fry them in hot oil. Be careful because the oil can spatter." She showed Jessie how to use tongs to put the dough in the oil. "When the doughnuts are nice and brown, we take them out and roll them in sugar."

"The most important part!" Benny said.

"I think the most important part is to taste them!" Henry teased.

While they were eating the crullers, Mrs. Vanderhoff said, "I want you all to enjoy yourselves while you're in town. Annika, why don't you take our guests to the Harvest Festival and the Halloween costume parade in the town square? There will be food booths and music and games. If you'd like to dress up in costumes, you might be able to find something in the attic to wear."

"We would like that," Jessie said. "There are some wonderful old clothes up there."

"I'll help you look for something," Annika said. "I might wear a costume too."

They hurried up to the attic, excited about the parade. "I feel bad that we have to leave Watch caged up while we're out having fun," Benny said.

"Watch can go too," Annika said as she opened one of the trunks. "Some people bring their dogs dressed up in costumes."

One trunk was full of colorful dresses covered in rows of fringe. There were headbands that matched, and each one had a big feather attached. "I think girls from the 1920s wore these sorts of dresses," Jessie said.

"That's right," Annika said. She put a blue headband on. "The girls who wore these dresses were called flappers."

"Flappers? That's funny," Benny said. "Did they do this?" He ran in a circle flapping his arms. Everyone laughed.

"Not like that," Jessie said, "but I want to be a flapper."

"Me too." Violet picked up a purple dress. "I'd like to wear this one." The dresses were too long for Jessie and Violet, so Mrs. McGregor helped them pin them up to the right length.

"This looks like a uniform." Henry put on a black jacket with gold stripes on the sleeves.

"That belonged to my grandfather," Annika said. "He was a pilot during World War II."

"Can I be a pilot too?" Benny asked.

Violet said, "I don't think there is another uniform. Even if there was, I'm afraid it wouldn't fit you."

Jessie picked up a battered brown hat. "You could wear this and be an explorer. I saw a man's brown shirt that matches. If we roll up the sleeves, you can wear that too."

"That's a good idea," Henry said. "I found an old metal water canteen. You could use that as part of the costume."

Once Benny had his costume together, Violet said, "Now that we all have costumes, what is Watch going to wear?"

"How about this bow tie and vest?" Jessie said. "He can be a dog professor."

When they were ready, they went downstairs to the shop. Mrs. McGregor clapped her hands at the sight of them. "You look wonderful! Let me take a picture to show your grandfather."

Downtown, they found crowds of people. "I smell something good," Benny said as they walked through the festival.

"The Apple House Café has a booth here," Annika told him. "You're smelling their apple custard tarts. They're famous for that."

"I'd like to try one," Benny said, "but only if Brett and Mr. Beekman aren't there. I don't like mean people."

"I don't see them." Violet stood on tiptoes so she could see over the crowd. "Some other people are working there."

Everyone tried the tarts.

"These are delicious." Jessie nibbled on hers slowly, tasting each bite. "I want to learn to make these too."

"Mr. Beekman is too mean to give you the recipe," Annika said. "I'll ask my mother if she knows how to make them. We should go say hello to Isiah. He's working in the library booth."

"That booth that says *library*," Benny said. "I see a girl dressed as an elf, but not Isiah."

Annika greeted the girl and asked, "Isn't Isiah supposed to be working?"

The girl slammed down a box of bookmarks. "Yes, but he didn't show up. I can't believe he didn't even call."

"He's been doing that too often," Annika said. "If I see him, I'll remind him he's supposed to be working. We should go. It's almost time for the parade."

"Look at those funny costumes." Benny pointed to some adults dressed as zoo animals walking by the booth. They were all carrying musical instruments.

"That's the band that leads the parade," Annika said. "We can follow them to the starting point. I wonder where Margot is. I thought she'd be here taking pictures. "

All the children and pets participating in the parade gathered at one end of the street. The band struck up a tune. The children began to march as the bystanders clapped for them.

They were halfway down the block when Violet stopped. "There's the headless horseman." She pointed up the street where a figure wearing a big black cape sat on a large black horse. It looked like there was no head above the cape.

"Maybe it's part of the parade," Henry suggested. "They could have someone dress up in costume to make the end of the parade more exciting."

"There's something strange about the horse," Jessie said. "It has red all around its eyes and mouth. And the coat is too shimmery for a normal horse."

Other children around them began to point as the horse and rider came closer. "That horse is scary," a little girl dressed as a fairy said.

Watch growled.

The horse reared up and gave an angry neigh.

CHAPTER 7

The Horseman Strikes Again

The musicians in front slowed down, and the music trailed off. The children behind them slowed too.

"I don't think that person is part of the event," Violet said.

The horse began to move toward them, slowly at first, just like on the ghost tour.

"I don't like this," Benny said.

The rider kicked the horse's sides until it broke into a run, charging right at them.

"Get out of the way!" Jessie gasped. Most

of the children and the musicians scattered off the street. But Jessie noticed that two smaller children weren't moving. They were too confused.

Jessie picked up the girl in the fairy costume and carried her to safety. Henry took hold of the little boy in a superhero costume. He led him to the sidewalk just as the rider drew close. The rider pulled the horse to a stop, reached under the cape and took out a white pumpkin.

The father of the little boy ran up and grabbed his son, taking him away into the crowd. Jessie looked around for a parent to claim the little girl she held in her arms. She heard a woman yelling, "Samantha! Where are you!"

"Mommy, I'm here," the girl cried.

Before Jessie could find the woman, Violet said, "Uh-oh. I know what's going to happen."

The horseman raised the pumpkin up and then tossed it toward them. The pumpkin hit the ground right in front of Jessie and Violet. It split open, and dark red liquid spattered out. The rider kicked the horse again rode away down a side street.

The girl Jessie held screamed and began to cry. Her mother came up and took her from Jessie. "It's okay," the woman told the girl, but she was crying too. "Thank you!" she said to Jessie.

A boy in a fireman costume held out his hand. "I'm bleeding!"

"No," Benny said. "It's just paint. See?" Benny took his finger and wiped off a speck of paint from the boy's hand.

"Are you all right?" Annika called as she hurried over to them. She looked over her shoulder and turned back to the Aldens. "The mayor doesn't look happy."

Henry turned to see a big man in a dark suit stomping across the street toward them.

The man stopped in front of Annika. "How could you arrange a trick like that?" he asked. "That is not the way to get business for your tours. Look how you've frightened the children with your stunts."

"It wasn't me," Annika protested. "I don't know who was riding that horse."

"You expect anyone to believe that?" The mayor shook his finger at her. "I don't want anything like this happening again. If it does, the town council might not let you use your wagon after all." He turned and walked away.

Annika called after him. "It really wasn't me!"

The mayor didn't respond.

"What did he mean about the wagon?" Jessie asked.

"I had to get special permission from the town council to use it in the woods. If the council changes their mind, I'll have to change the whole tour. The wagon ride is one of the best parts of it. I don't know what to do."

"We have to find out who is playing these tricks and make them stop," Jessie said.

"Let's see if we can find any clues," Henry suggested. "I wish we had thought to run after the horse to see where they went."

"I don't think you're going to find any clues," Annika said. "There won't be any footprints on the street to follow."

"You might be surprised," Benny said. "We're good at finding clues."

The four of them walked to where they

had first seen the horse. They searched up and down for anything that could be a clue. The street was empty.

They were ready to give up when Jessie cried, "I found something!" She brushed her finger across a lamppost. When she held it up, they could see it was covered with something black and glittering. "The horse must have brushed against the post, and this is what made it all shimmery."

Violet touched her sister's finger. "It's a little sticky, like glitter glue."

Benny pointed at something on the street a few feet away. "What's that? He darted forward and picked it up. "It's a sugar cube, like the ones we saw at the café."

"Why would anyone carry sugar cubes?" Violet asked.

"I don't know, but it's a clue," Henry said. "Let's go tell Annika."

Before they could tell her, Margot came rushing up. "I can't believe I missed all that! How exciting! I hope my boss got pictures of it."

"Margot, it was terrible," Annika said.

"The mayor thinks I arranged it. I told him I didn't, but I don't think he believes me."

"Oh, don't worry about the mayor." Margot smiled. "As soon as we win the contest, he'll be happy about anything that helps the town seem scary. He'll even thank you." She waved at someone in the crowd. "There's my boss. I'll see you later."

"I'm ready to go home," Annika said. "The festival is ruined for me."

Back at the Vanderhoffs', Jessie got her notebook again. "We can't take anyone off our list with this latest trick. Brett, Mr. Beckman, Margo, and Isiah were not at the parade when the horseman appeared. Any one of them could have been the rider."

"We aren't making much progress," Violet said.

"I think we should look for clues on the ghost walk," Henry suggested. "And we should go now when there is still daylight."

"Good idea," Jessie said. "There have to be more clues somewhere."

"We can bring Watch," Benny said. "He'd like a walk."

They found the starting point for the ghost tour and walked down the path into the woods. "It isn't scary during the daytime," Benny said. "How are we going to know where we first saw the horse and the rider?"

"We had been walking a while," Henry said. "I remember the path went around a bend a little ways before we saw the horseman."

They found the right spot and searched carefully but didn't find anything.

"I think there are too many leaves." Benny scuffed through some. "And too many people have been walking through here."

"I'm sorry we didn't find anything, but it is very pretty here," Violet said. "I'd like to come back and sketch this part of the path. Look at that big tree. I like how the branch hangs over the path." She pointed and then lowered her arm, frowning. "There's something up in that tree that doesn't belong there."

CHAPTER 8

Missing

"I don't see anything," Jessie said.

"It's right above the big branch." Violet walked under the tree and pointed. "That black thing."

"I see it." Henry went over to the tree trunk. "I think I can climb up there." He found enough handholds and footholds to get up in the tree, and finally he crawled along the branch over the path.

He stopped and held up a short black plastic tube. "This is interesting," he said.

"It's tied to the branch." He reached inside, and withdrew two red glowing circles like big scary eyes.

"How did you do that?" Benny asked.

"There are two holes cut in this pipe." Henry lowered it down so it hung over the path. "Inside is a red glow stick with an on off switch."

"So that's how someone made it look like the horse had big glowing eyes," Jessie said. "It wasn't on the horse at all. Someone reached up and took it down when they rode the horse under it."

"We can take it and show Annika," Benny said.

"Why don't we leave it here and keep watch to see who is using it," Henry suggested. "If someone tried to scare Annika's tour once, he or she will probably do it again."

"But that means we'd have to wait in the woods in the dark." Benny looked around at the trees. "I don't know if I want to do that."

"You wouldn't have to, Benny." Jessie hugged him. "You could go on the tour with Annika. Let's go tell her the plan."

They hurried back to the house and told Annika about the glow stick and explained their plan to find out who was using it.

"That's a terrible trick," she said. "I don't know who would go to that much trouble to scare my groups. I have some other bad news. The people who were supposed to go on the tour tonight canceled. They have small children and they said they heard it was too scary. I'll never earn enough money for a new roof now."

"What about tomorrow night? Are some people scheduled to go on the tour then?"

"There are," Annika said. "If they don't cancel."

"You're worrying too much," Mrs. Vanderhoff said. "We'll manage somehow. I don't want you to spend your time dwelling on these tricks. I want you to have fun too. Why don't you take our guests to see a play? A theater group in town has turned the *Legend of Sleepy Hollow* story into a play."

Annika was quiet for a moment and then said, "That's a good idea. You've all been trying so hard to help me that I feel bad your vacation hasn't been more fun. I'll call Isiah too. He'll want to go see the play now that the tour has been canceled."

They met Isiah in front of the theater. He wasn't dressed in a costume, but he was wearing an old-fashioned brown suit with a brown hat.

"I like your fedora," Violet told him. "Old hats are fun to wear."

"Thank you," Isiah said. "I've got a whole hat collection. I've also got tickets for all of us." He handed everyone one a ticket.

When they had gone inside and found their seats, Jessie looked around. She saw a familiar face.

"Isn't that Brett?" she asked Annika. "That man next to the stage wearing headphones?"

"Yes," Annika said. "When we were in high school, Brett and his friends did the sound and lighting for the school plays. I don't like Brett, but he was good at that work. I didn't know he was helping the theater group."

"Is this play going to be scary?" Benny asked.

"A little," Henry said. "It's just a play

though. The headless horseman scares a man named Ichabod Crane."

"Ichabod? That's a very funny name," Benny said.

"Ichabod is a good part. I should have been cast," Isiah said. "I tried out for the play, but I didn't get the part. I think Brett convinced the director the role should go to one of his friends."

The lights in the theater dimmed and the play started. Several times during the show, the spooky sounds and lights startled the audience. When a big dark shadow that looked like a headless horseman chased Ichabod Crane, Benny whispered to Jessie, "This is not just a little scary, it's very scary."

After the play was done and the lights came back on, Jessie said, "That was very good. I felt like I was right in the forest."

"I did too," Violet said. "Even though there wasn't a real horse, that shadow made me afraid."

Annika said, "I have to admit Brett and his friends did a good job with the sounds and lights."

"Don't tell him that," Isiah said. "It'll go to his head, and his head is big enough already."

"It looks like a normal size to me." Benny sounded puzzled.

Everyone else laughed. "Having a big head means someone thinks they are better than everyone else," Jessie explained.

They were putting on their coats when someone behind Isiah yelled "Boo!"

Everyone jumped.

It was Brett. He laughed and slapped Isiah on the shoulder. "Isiah, you are still as jumpy as ever. I remember how scared you used to be when the theater went dark. When you go home tonight, you should watch out. You never know what's waiting for you." He laughed again and turned away.

"Brett and his friends need to grow up," Jessie said.

"They do," Isiah agreed. "They used to think it was funny to turn off the lights in the theater when no one expected it. It wasn't funny to anyone else."

"Just ignore him," Annika said.

Outside the theater, the wind had picked

up. It blew the fallen leaves into swirling patterns. Rain began to fall.

"Annika, can you give me a ride?" Isiah asked. "My car broke down."

"Of course," she said.

"How did you get here?" Henry asked.

"I walked through the cemetery, but it wasn't dark and stormy then. I'd rather not go back that way."

They were almost at Annika's car when Isiah stopped and patted his pocket. "Oh no. My cell phone is missing. It must have fallen out of my pocket inside the theater. I'll have to go back and look for it. You go on."

"We can wait for you," Annika said.

"No, I don't know how long it will take me to find it. I'll just get a ride from someone else. I'll see you tomorrow." He went back inside.

"Not again," Annika said. She shook her head and said to the Aldens, "Let's hurry to the car. I don't want to get soaked."

The Aldens and Annika got back to the Vanderhoffs' just as it began the rain began to fall very hard.

The storm got worse as the Aldens were getting ready for bed.

As they lay there listening to the thunder and lightning, Jessie said, "I hope Isiah got a ride. I wouldn't want to be outside in this. Maybe we should have waited for him."

"I hope he at least found his phone," Henry said. "I've never known anyone who loses things so much or has so many things go wrong. Remember that first night when he had a flat tire and lost his cell phone then too?"

"He also said the wagon wheel broke," Jessie added. "Then the night the horse nearly ran us down on the ghost tour, Isiah said he fell down and that's how he got muddy." She told them how she noticed there wasn't any mud around the carriage that night.

"Is Isiah lying about some of the things he claims happened to him?" Benny asked.

"I don't know," Violet said, "but all those things are suspicious." She yawned. "Let's talk in the morning. I think I can fall asleep now."

***

The next morning the Aldens helped Mrs.

Vanderhoff in the shop while they were waiting for the ghost tour to start.

After lunch, Annika said, "I'd better call Isiah and make sure he knows we have a tour tonight." She dialed and listened for a few moments before hanging up. "He's not answering."

"Maybe he couldn't find his phone," Jessie suggested.

"Yes. Knowing Isiah, he could have lost it anywhere," Annika said. "I guess I should go to his apartment and tell him in person. Would you all like to come with me? I want to treat you to some ice cream for all your hard work."

"We'll always say yes ice cream," Benny said. The rest of the Aldens agreed.

Isiah lived in an apartment in a big old house overlooking the cemetery. Annika rang the bell and the landlady came to the door. Annika explained they were looking for Isiah.

"You can knock on his door," the landlady told them. "But I don't think he's there. I haven't seen him since yesterday afternoon. His car has been here all night, but he hasn't."

"That's strange," Annika said.

"There's something else that's odd," the landlady said. "I found one of his hats in the back of the yard by the cemetery this morning." She picked up a hat from a table next to the door. It was the brown fedora Isiah had worn the night before.

"You would think he'd notice his hat fell off," Violet said.

"Maybe he couldn't get a ride after all," Henry suggested. "He could have been hurrying through the cemetery to get home because of the rain. The wind was blowing very hard last night."

"I'll call the library," Annika said. She took out her phone and dialed. She asked the person on the other end a few questions and frowned when she hung up. "He's not supposed to work today. They haven't seen him. I hope he shows up later. I don't know how I'll do the tour without the wagon. I'll call his parents. They live in town." She made another phone call.

Henry, Jessie, Violet, and Benny exchanged glances. They could tell Annika was becoming concerned.

When she hung up, her face was pale. "No one has seen or heard from him. Isiah is missing."

CHAPTER 9

Mystery in the Woods

"Isiah's father says he'll turn up, but I'm worried," Annika said. "I have to cancel the tour now. I don't have anyone else to drive the wagon."

"I have an idea," Henry said. "If you drive the wagon to the pickup spot and left it there with us, we could watch over it until you arrive."

"That would be a big help." Annika smiled. "The horses are very gentle and well-trained. They won't give you any problems."

When it was time, Annika drove the Aldens to the stable. It was a long white building on the edge of town. When they pulled up in front of it, Henry said, "The sign says Sanders Stables. Does it belong to Isiah?"

"No, it belongs to Isiah's father." Annika got out of the car. "He has several horses they use for tourist trail rides and wagon rides. That's how I'm able to borrow one of their wagons."

"Could this be where the mystery horse lives?" Jessie asked. "It has to have a stable close to town."

"If it's a real horse," Benny said, "and not an evil spirit horse."

"It's a real horse," Violet said. "I'm sure of it."

"There's no all-black horse at the stable," Annika assured them. "I would have recognized it. I've been riding horses here for years."

A tall older man who looked a little like Isiah was feeding the horses inside. "Hello, Mr. Sanders. These are my friends." Annika introduced everyone.

"Isiah still hasn't shown up," Mr. Sanders told them.

"We'll manage without him," Annika said. "I need to hitch up the horses a bit early and get the wagon in place. If you do see Isiah, will you tell him to come to the meeting place?"

Mr. Sanders said he would.

"How many horses do you have here, Mr. Sanders?" Henry asked.

"About twenty. Some are too old to do more than loaf around most of the time." He rubbed the nose of the brown horse he was feeding.

A black-and-white horse at the end of the stalls stuck his head over the wall and looked at them.

"That's a pretty horse," Violet said.

Mr. Sanders snorted. "I've never thought of Domino as pretty. He's always had a bad temper and he bites. The older he gets, the crankier he acts. Isiah is the only one he likes because Isiah gives him treats. Too bad he's not like Ghost and Spook. They are good horses. Now let's get that wagon ready."

Ghost and Spook stood patiently while

Annika and Mr. Sanders showed the Aldens how to fasten the harnesses.

"Henry, if you'd like to drive the wagon, I'll show you how," Annika said. "We take the back roads so there aren't many cars."

Henry took the reins and drove the wagon along the back roads of Sleepy Hollow to the right spot.

Annika and the Aldens got down and fastened the reins to a tree. Annika pulled something out of her pocket. "Ghost and Spook should be fine, but if they get restless, just feed them a few of these." She held out some sugar cubes. "Sugar isn't good for them, but Isiah says it's all right once in a while." Ghost whinnied at the sight of the treats. "He loves them," Annika said. "Do you know how to feed a horse a treat?"

"Yes," Jessie said. "You hold your hand out flat with the treat in your palm."

"That's right. You don't want a horse thinking your fingers are a snack. They might nibble on them. Now I have to get my car and go home and change. Are you sure you'll be okay?"

"We're sure," Henry assured her.

As Annika hurried off, she said over her shoulder, "Just call me with your cell phone if you need anything."

Jessie petted Ghost's nose. Her brothers and sister could tell she was thinking about something.

"What are you thinking about?" Violet asked.

"At least we know that horse at the parade was not a ghost horse," she replied. "That sugar cube Benny found was a treat for him. Spirit horses don't eat treats."

"You're right," Henry said. "We should check the tube. It's going to be dark soon."

They walked down the path. Fallen leaves crunched beneath their feet, but otherwise the woods were silent.

"It is colder than it was last night," Violet said, pulling her hat down on her head.

"It's getting dark faster than I thought it would," Henry said. "We should hurry."

A loud crack came from down the path, and then a groaning noise. The Aldens froze in place. They waited, but there were no other sounds.

"What do we do?" Violet whispered.

"We keep going," Henry said. "That sounded like a human groan, not a ghost groan."

They crept as quietly as they could down the path. "It's just around this bend," Jessie said.

They came to the big tree. "The tube is still there." Benny pointed out it.

"I see something is different." Henry walked over to the trunk. "That branch wasn't broken before. I used it to get up in the tree."

"Maybe a big animal crashed into it and broke it," Violet said.

Henry shook his head. "Look where it broke, along the top, just like when someone is climbing a tree and the branch won't hold them. When that happens, it breaks at the trunk first."

"So that means someone was climbing up the tree," Jessie said.

Benny fell to the ground. "And he fell down like this!"

"And then he groaned because it hurt,"

Violet added. "But whoever did it ran off. Let's see if we can find some clues to tell us which way he or she ran."

While they were looking, Henry's cell phone rang. Annika was calling. He put her on speaker so they could all hear. "Everyone has canceled their spots on the tour." She sounded very upset. "I'll be there soon to help bring the wagon back. We won't be able to find out who is playing the tricks tonight after all."

"I don't think anyone will try tonight." Henry explained about the broken branch. "We think whoever is playing tricks fell and got hurt."

"We may never solve this mystery," Annika said and sighed. "I'll be there soon."

When she arrived, they took the horses back to the stable and then drove to the Vanderhoffs'. Margot was outside by the fire with Mrs. Vanderhoff and Mrs. McGregor. She was very interested to hear the story of the broken branch and the tube. "Whoever is doing that is very clever," she said.

"It may be clever, but it's not very nice," Violet said.

Jessie went to get her notebook. She brought it back to the fire and sat down. "I've been thinking. Are there other stables around town where the mystery horse could live?"

Margot shuddered. "Don't ask me. I don't keep track of the horses in town."

"You don't like horses?" Violet asked.

"Not at all." Margot shuddered again. "They're so big that they could trample you if they got angry. I should be going. Busy day tomorrow. Let me know if you see or hear anything else that's scary."

After Margot left, Mrs. Vanderhoff explained, "Margot has been frightened of horses ever since she was a little girl. A horse stepped on her foot one time."

"So I guess that means she doesn't ride horses," Henry said.

Annika laughed. "She certainly doesn't. She wouldn't even ride a horse on a merry-go-round."

Benny yawned. "I'm getting sleepy. Ghost tours even without ghosts make me tired."

"It's time for bed." Jessie closed her

notebook. "We'll make a new plan in the morning."

When the Aldens were inside the apartment, Henry said, "At least we know Margot didn't play the tricks. If she's so scared of horses, she's not the rider."

"That leaves Isiah, Mr. Beekman, or Brett." Violet went to the window and looked out into the dark. "One of them is still out there planning more tricks."

CHAPTER 10

Help from a Horse

The next morning after breakfast, the Aldens helped Annika rake leaves and clean up outside the front of the shop. They saw Mr. Beekman struggling to carry a big box up the steps of the café. His ankle was wrapped in a bandage.

"Let me help you," Henry offered, hurrying to the café.

Mr. Beekman looked surprised, but said, "Thank you. I was afraid I was going to drop it."

Mrs. Vanderhoff came out of the shop. "Mr. Beekman, what happened to your ankle?" she asked.

"I sprained it when I tripped over a broken step in back," he said.

"You should get one of your workers to carry things in," Mrs. Vanderhoff scolded. "The ankle won't get better unless you rest it."

Mr. Beekman shook his head. "I can't. They're all busy with other jobs. We're having a special charity dinner tonight to raise money for the library."

"We can help," Jessie offered.

"Yes," Mrs. Vanderhoff added. "We'll all help. Just tell us what you want us to do."

Mr. Beekman frowned and asked, "Why would you help me?"

"I like to be neighborly," replied Mrs. Vanderhoff. "And I'm happy to do anything that helps the library."

Mr. Beekman took his volunteers to the backyard. Mrs. Vanderhoff and Mrs. McGregor set the tables that had been placed there while Jessie, Henry, and Annika helped string paper lanterns around the trees. Violet and Benny did the centerpieces. Benny scattered colorful leaves on the table and Violet arranged miniature pumpkins and pinecones around small pots of yellow mums.

When they were done, Mr. Beekman said, "I can't thank you enough. I couldn't have done it without you." He turned to Mrs. Vanderhoff. "I want to apologize. Ever since you said you weren't selling your house, I haven't been very nice to you. I realize how unkind that is."

"Apology accepted." Mrs. Vanderhoff gave him a big smile.

"Why don't you all come in for a snack?" Mr. Beekman said.

Mrs. Vanderhoff and the Aldens followed him inside and sat down at a table. He brought them hot chocolate and a plate of his apple custard tarts.

"Hello!" Isiah called out from the front door of the café. He came over to their table and did a funny little dance like a jig. "It's a wonderful day. I have some wonderful news."

"Where have you been?" Annika asked.

Isiah pointed at himself. "You are looking at an actor who has a real part in a real play in New York City. I found out the other night. I took the train into the city right away so I could sign the contract."

"Congratulations!" Annika said. "But you could have told someone," she grumbled. "We've been worried."

"I couldn't find my cell phone, but I left you a note. I taped to the front door of the shop."

"We didn't see any note," Mrs. Vanderhoff said. "It must have blown away."

While Isiah was telling Annika about the play, Henry pulled the rest of the Aldens aside. "So now we know it wasn't Isiah and it wasn't Margot. That leaves Mr. Beekman or Brett."

"Mr. Beekman said he fell down the steps, but he could have sprained his ankle falling out of a tree," Jessie said.

"Brett is the meanest one though," Violet said. "I think it was him."

"How are we going to find out which one it is?" Benny asked as he reached over to take a sugar cube out of the bowl.

"Benny, your hot chocolate doesn't need anymore sugar!" Jessie said.

Henry took a sugar cube of his own. "This gives me an idea," he said. "Anyone else guess what I'm thinking? Benny isn't the only one who likes sugar cubes."

Violet nodded. "I bet I can guess what your idea is."

Henry got up and went over to Mr. Beekman. "Could you and Brett do us a big favor?"

"Of course," Mr. Beekman said. "You've helped me out. I'll help you out."

"We need you to come to Sanders Stable, just for a few minutes," Henry said. "I'll explain there."

Mr. Beekman looked very puzzled but agreed to go. He went to get Brett, who did not seem pleased at Henry's request.

When they all reached the stable, Isiah's father was outside washing out brushes.

"We just need to see the horses for few minutes," Jessie told him.

"I usually don't have folks come just to visit the horses, but you're welcome to come in." He showed them inside. Domino looked out of his stall and neighed at the sight of them. Mr. Sanders frowned. "I wonder what's gotten into him."

"Let's go see," Violet suggested.

They walked down to the end of the row of stalls. Henry motioned to the front of Domino's stall. "Mr. Beekman and Brett, would you just stand together right here?"

"I don't know why you want us to do that, but I guess you'll tell us soon enough," Mr. Beekman said.

The Beekmans moved into place.

Domino stuck his head out and butted it against Brett's chest, whinnying softly.

"I don't believe it," Mr. Sanders said. "I think he likes you."

"Why don't you give him a treat?" Henry said, taking some sugar cubes from his pocket. He tried to hand one to Brett, but Brett wouldn't take it.

Domino neighed, sounding angry.

"I think you should give the horse the treat," Mr. Sanders said. "When Domino gets angry, sometimes he kicks the stall door."

"Go ahead, Brett," Mr. Beekman said.

Brett fed Domino the sugar cube. The horse rubbed his nose against Brett's chest and whinnied again. "He acts like he knows you," Mr. Sanders said.

Brett didn't say anything but he looked uncomfortable.

"Mr. Sanders, could we see where you keep the grooming supplies?" Jessie asked.

"They're in the tack room." He opened the door to a small room across from Domino's stall. "The brushes are drying outside, but most of the other supplies are in that cabinet."

"May I look in the cabinet?" Violet asked.

Mr. Sanders nodded. Violet opened it and examined the containers and jars. She reached in and took out a jar full of black glittery gel.

Mr. Sanders took a step back in surprise. "I don't know how that got in there. People use that on horses in parades and horse shows. We don't have any need for that here."

Violet pulled out two cans. "These say horse paint. There is one can of black and one can of red."

"Isiah, did you put the paint there?" Mr. Sanders asked.

Isiah shook his head. The Aldens all looked at Brett.

Brett's face turned red. "I did," he admitted. "I've been dressing up as a headless horseman and borrowing Domino. I used the paint and the glitter to make him black and frightening."

"Did you do all the other tricks too?" Henry asked. "The tube with the eyes in the woods?"

"Yes," Brett said. "And I hurt my wrist yesterday when I was trying to climb the tree."

"What about the fake worms and dirt in the cookie jar?" Jessie asked. "Did you do that too?"

He ducked his head. "I did that too. I'm very, very sorry."

"Brett, how could you?" Mr. Beekman was shocked and angry.

"I wanted the Vanderhoffs to sell their house so we could buy it. I don't always want to be a waiter."

"That's no excuse for all you've done," Mr. Beekman said. "Mr. Sanders could call the police. You've been stealing his horse."

Mr. Sanders sat down on a stool. "I can't say I understand exactly what's going on, but since the horse is back here in his stall, there's no need to call the police. He doesn't look like he's been harmed."

"Brett will pay you for the time he was riding him though, the regular rental fee." Mr. Beekman said.

"Well, right now I need something more than money. I could use more help mucking out these stalls. Especially since Isiah will be spending more time in New York City."

"I'll see that he's here whenever you need him." Mr. Beekman turned to Annika. "And he'll make it up to you too."

Before Annika could answer, her cell phone rang. She answered, and when she hung up a few moments later, she was smiling. "I can hardly believe it. That was Margot. They've been getting calls at the office from people wanting to go on the haunted ghost tour they've heard about. People who want to be scared! I guess I'll have to change my tours."

"I can help," Brett said. "I know that won't make up for all the tricks I played, but it will be a start. I'm good at thinking up ways to scare people."

"Yes, you are," Violet and Benny said together. Everyone laughed.

"I don't know." Annika frowned. "You'll have to stop being mean to Isiah."

"I will, I promise. And I'll think up tricks that not even the Aldens will be able to figure out."

"I wouldn't count on that," Mrs. Vanderhoff said. "I suspect Sleepy Hollow wouldn't be very spooky if the Aldens lived here. They'd solve all our hauntings and mysteries."

"We'd be happy to try," Jessie said.

Mr. Beekman looked at his watch. "Before the Aldens take on another mystery, I'd like you all to be my guests at the library dinner tonight. It's starting soon. Mr. Sanders and Isiah too. The Alden detectives deserve a feast after all their hard work."

"We did work hard, didn't we?" Benny said. "I knew there was a reason I'm so hungry. Let's go!"

The adventures continue in the newest mysteries!

THE

BOXCAR
CHILDREN

HIDDEN IN THE HAUNTED SCHOOL

Created by
GERTRUDE CHANDLER WARNER

PB ISBN: 9780807507193, $5.99

THE ELECTION DAY DILEMMA

SAVE THE TOWN!
VOTE
for
ALBERT HUND

SAVE THE TOWN!
VOTE
for
ALBERT HUND

SAVE TH
VO
for
ALBER

Vote For
Alice Wells
Alden

Alice Wells
Alden

Created by
GERTRUDE CHANDLER WARNER

PB ISBN: 9780807507223, $5.99

GERTRUDE CHANDLER WARNER discovered when she was teaching that many readers who like an exciting story could find no books that were both easy and fun to read. She decided to try to meet this need, and her first book, *The Boxcar Children*, quickly proved she had succeeded.

Miss Warner drew on her own experiences to write the mystery. As a child she spent hours watching trains go by on the tracks opposite her family home. She often dreamed about what it would be like to set up housekeeping in a caboose or freight car—the situation the Alden children find themselves in.

While the mystery element is central to each of Miss Warner's books, she never thought of them as strictly juvenile mysteries. She liked to stress the Aldens' independence and resourcefulness and their solid New England devotion to using up and making do. The Aldens go about most of their adventures with as little adult supervision as possible—something else that delights young readers.

Miss Warner lived in Putnam, Connecticut, until her death in 1979. During her lifetime, she received hundreds of letters from girls and boys telling her how much they liked her books.